FOUND KNIGHTS... LOST DAYS

ROSIE O'NEILL

LITTLE FLOWER TRADING COMPANY LLC

This book is dedicated to my late husband,
Alex Tangredi.
I will love you forever.
XOXOXOXOXOXO

ACKNOWLEDGEMENTS

First, I have to thank my family. My parents, James and Margaret O'Neill, and their parents, John and Bridget O'Donnell and James and Catherine O'Neill, were wonderful people. They gave and continue to give their love unselfishly to me, my siblings and our extended family. They supported all our endeavors and are the inspiration for *Found Knights... Lost Days*. Their stories about life in Ireland shaped my childhood and now have helped to shape this book. My parents and grandparents encouraged me to pursue my dreams and taught me that I could accomplish everything my heart desired.

My siblings, Catherine, Jimmy, John, Eddie, Bucky, Peggy, Gerry, Owen and my twin, Anne, are all living proof that they are products of my parents and grandparents.

My sibling's spouses and children have and are still carrying on the kindness and goodness. Additionally, life would be nothing without loving aunts, uncles and cousins. All separate, but together we are one. (How did one family get so many A type personalities?!)

Thank you, Aunt Dorothy, for being my first reader and fan. (Now you know the ending!)

To all the historians and researchers of Ireland, Donegal, Bishop O'Donnell, St Eunan's, London, Croatia, Houdini, Theodore Roosevelt, the Courrières mine disaster and many other items... your hard work and how you passed it on, made this book possible. Thank you so very much.

Thank you to my dear sister, Catherine, and her husband Bill, who were the most awesome beta readers anyone could ask to have. Your attention to detail made so much of this book possible.

Thank you to the people of the hamlet of Wading River, New York - a magical place which included Second and 1/2 Street, a bunny trail, "the" big rock, Clay Mountain, "the" mansion, Barberry Park, Wildwood State Park, the 2x4 restaurant, duck ponds, and many other memorable places and landmarks. Wading River was a town like no other.

I grew up surrounded by wonderful families who made our little slice of heaven a joyous place to live. There were many people who provided love and support during my "growing up" years. Special thanks to the following families: Johannemann, Wagner, Schwartzmeir, Soto, O'Shea, Fontana, Wynne, Amaro, Doelger, Witt, Tallon, Turpin, Oliveri, Kerrigan, Loughlin, Lopez and the members of The Sound Shore Club.

To Margaret and James O'Neill, Fran and Ed Johannemann, and Rose and Michael O'Shea... you were examples of genuine faith and love for your families. Seeing how you believed and gave to others has never left me. You helped to shape this book.

To Mary Kelly, one of the most wonderful people I know, you taught me so much about faith and moving on after adversity. I will love you always.

To Mrs. Elaine W. Kelsey... you were a remarkable English teacher in high school and you have been a monumental friend in life. I cherish you and your sons. (Now, let's pick out a wine!)

A remembrance to Michael and Marion Dorman, who were teachers and residents in the Riverhead, New York area. You touched many lives. I wanted to make sure the rest of the world knew you were here.

Thank you to Donna Carbone , owner of Write for You, LLC. She is a wonderful and gifted writer and editor and a damned nice person. With great effort, she got me away from overusing *just* and *then*. There would have been no book without her. You cannot know Donna without knowing her kind and caring husband, Dr.

Michael Carbone. The two of you bring good wherever you go. (We are still meeting on Thursdays!)

Thanks to the Palm Beach Institute for Entertainment and Arts... a non-profit that does wonderful things for their community.

Thank you to Chris Hall, who designed the cover for this book. I will be forever grateful for the day we met. Who knew it would be because of your superb rum - Noxx & Dunn!

To the late Agnes Nixon... you were a master storyteller. The soap operas you created - *All My Children* and *One Life to Live* - were education through entertainment.

To my dear late friend, Bernadette Clyne, I miss you so. I am so glad we were friends. Your love of your native Ireland and its people and your kindness is now known to all. (Now, let's go have a drink!)

Thank you to Astrologer Maria DiSimone. You told me it was in my stars to write. So, I did.

To my cats, GeorgeElvis and Trelmarie. You are the greatest. I will now have a little more time for you again. (Yes, I have treats)

Thank you to Dr Predrag Knez. You are the kindest and most gifted healer I know. You heal so much more than people's hearts. I will always be grateful to you. (Hi, hubba, hubba.)

Lastly, to my late husband, Alex. Mr. T, you were one of a kind. Thank you for all of the great years. I can still hear your voice encouraging me. Thanks for watching out for me. (I hope the Yankees and Steelers win. ☺)

XOXOXOXOXOXOXOXOX

CHAPTER ONE

"I have always been delighted at the prospect of a new day, a fresh try, one more start, with perhaps a bit of magic behind the morning."
~ J. B. Priestly ~

*T*here was peace in the valley.

From the time the meteors first impacted the earth and created what are today's oceans, there has been tremendous unrest. At first, the waters boiled and steamed, making them unstable, untouchable and uninhabitable. These waters were vast but how vast would remain unknown until the temperature cooled. Below the restless waters, microscopic life was evolving. Some transmuted into the creatures we know today, while others exist only in stories about extinct species.

Peace was a state of mind and a place known as trident Valley, located off the south coast of Ireland. The closest landfall was the Blasket Islands, off the Dingle Peninsula. Here, in the deep undersea waters, was the habitat of the Merfolk. The Merfolk of Ireland were a binary species, having both Merman and

Mermaids. Much like humans, they were born young and grew old; they were born small and grew large.

Their home was near the bottom of the Valley in which an undersea river ebbed and flowed. The Merfolk called it Wading River (Abhainn Wading in Gaelic) for it was here they went for relaxation and physical therapy using the water's natural currents, its healing waters, atoms and molecules.

The Merfolk referred to themselves as the tridents of Wading River. They were fluent in both Gaelic, the only language spoken in The Blasket Islands, and English. The older generation tended to speak only Gaelic, while the younger generation spoke both. The tridents of Wading River were a gentle and peaceful tribe.

If someone was to take a leisurely swim around the hamlet of Wading River, they would encounter the merfolk who live in the region, as well as a myriad of sea life and the remnants of lost voyages from days gone by. On the floor of the Atlantic Ocean in this part of the world are sailing vessels from when man first began exploring the seas. Swimming as fast as the common or bottle nosed dolphins and the cod and mackerel, there would be younger Merboys and Mergirls using different areas of the valley and sea bottom as a playground.

At a more relaxed pace, swimmers would see humpback whales and basking sharks, as well as younger merfolk by themselves or with family. Crawling about the sandy floor would be crabs and starfish. Among the bottom dwellers would be more Merfolk... those males who searched for old whale bones and wood which would be whittled into keepsakes for their beloved.

The elder Merfolk were treated with the utmost respect by the younger generations. The elders were a conduit to the past; they possessed the knowledge needed to deal with the future. The ocean's seabed was an encyclopedia filled with many stories and riddles, as well as the answers to many questions humans longed to understand. The Merfolk took great pride in being the guardians of Neptune's secrets.

The peace in the valley was due to the anticipation felt at the soon-to-be birth of Glenn's and Muriel's first child. Glenn was the handsome bearded red-haired son of Proteus and Salacia. Proteus and Salacia were descendants of the many-generations-old tridents of Wading River.

Muriel was a dark-haired beauty... the daughter of Irwyn and Mirasol. Irwyn and Mirasol were new to the valley, having arrived after a shipwrecked schooner caused the collapse of their former home.

Glenn was revered by many in Wading River and not only because his parents and grandparents were outstanding citizens. As he grew from boy to man, he displayed a deep understanding of the needs of others based on his feelings. Glenn's intuitive nature was a gift to all who knew him. As a young child, he was able to sense terrible events before they happened. One such incident was a shipwreck off of the Blasket Islands.

As Glenn told the story, that particular day he had felt a nervousness in his stomach as he swam in the ocean waters during a thunderstorm. He was drawn out farther into the roiling seas and, there, he saw a young boy struggling to swim up to the ocean top. The ship in which he had been sailing was broken in pieces. No other humans could be seen. Glenn swam under the child, pushing his head above the waves, and guided him to the shore. He stayed with the boy, pumping water out of his lungs, until more humans arrived. Then, he disappeared back into the sea undetected.

When a teenager, Glenn had an encounter with a male bottle nosed dolphin. The dolphin began to swim in circles around Glenn, nudging him with his snout. Glenn realized he was expressing the need for help, so he followed the cetacean to where another dolphin was trapped in an abandoned fishing net.

Knowing that a dolphin's time underwater is limited to 10 minutes, Glenn worked at a furious pace to free the entangled creature before it would drown. As the freed dolphin and its mate swam away, Glenn realized that the female was pregnant. The male turned back to Glenn, once again circling him but this time making clicking sounds of glee. When Glenn stopped swimming, the dolphin came up close to his face and planted what could only be called a kiss upon his cheek.

When a child, Glenn's hair was a blazing red color, which distinguished him from many other lads in the Valley. He could always be seen trailing after his father, shadowing him wherever he went and copying his every move. As he got older, his youthful good looks became those of a strikingly handsome man.

His hair, which turned a rich sanguine color, matched his personality. He was an extrovert... highly talkative and exuberant. Glenn was always an optimist no matter how dire a situation. While time with his family was important to him, he sought out every opportunity to explore the world in which he dwelled, always learning from what he saw and the things he found.

Muriel was a kind soul... a born caregiver. From the time she was old enough to swim without the accompaniment of her parents, she had been drawn to the dry land. She had a special affection for the human children who played along the shoreline and would leave a scattering of shells and sea glass for them to find. She loved sharing her world with them, a world that they would otherwise never know existed.

A lovely child from the moment of birth, Muriel grew into a breathtakingly beautiful Merwoman. Her auburn locks, which framed her face in soft ginger-toned curls and undulating ripples of gold flecks was the envy of every female in the Valley. Her little girl giggles filled her parents' hearts with pure joy, and her kind and giving nature made her a favorite with all the Merfolk.

Glenn and Muriel shared a fascination for all the life forms who lived on the land, especially the two-legged creatures they saw along the shore. They enjoyed spying on the humans, who were smaller than Merfolk. The human's unrestrained joy, which was obvious as they ran and played on the soil and grass, aroused their curiosity.

The first time Glenn and Muriel saw each other was on a day when they had each decided to go exploring near the land. They were approaching a cliff that was lower to the water than most when they became aware that the other was nearby. Muriel began to swim away, but Glenn, being a more powerful swimmer, was able to reach her side quickly. He introduced himself. Muriel was very shy, but Glenn instantly knew she was his true love.

Once Muriel relaxed enough to respond to Glenn's questions, they realized they were headed in the same direction for the same reason. They were both tridents of Wading River. Knowing this filled Muriel with confidence. They swam together until they reached a wider part of the river where they would need to part ways. Glenn wished Muriel a safe journey home, knowing they would see each other again.

CHAPTER TWO

"There is only one happiness in this life, to love and be loved."
~ George Sand ~

*W*hen Glenn arrived home, he asked his parents if they were any new families in the valley. They were aware of the arrival of Irwyn and Mirasol, who had a daughter named Muriel. Proteus and Salacia wanted to know why their son was so inquisitive. He explained that he had met Muriel.

Proteus and Salacia knew from the tone of Glenn's voice and his demeanor that their son was taken with this girl. They asked how the meeting had come about, and Glenn explained that both he and Muriel had been watching the humans frolic on a cliff near to the Blasket Islands.

Proteus suddenly became angry with his son. Many times, had he warned Glenn to stay away from that area. Sea serpents, which posed a danger to all creatures, lurked in that area. He told Glenn that he would advise Irwyn and Mirasol to warn their daughter of the same danger.

In the time that followed, Glenn found himself swimming up and down along the river bank searching for Muriel. While there were many attractive girls in the Valley, none could compare to her. Glenn was determined to travel the seven seas, if necessary, to find Muriel. As chance would have it, he found her the next day.

Muriel was again reticent, but Glenn was like no other Merman she had encountered. His chivalrous gestures and offers to show her around the Valley gave her the feeling of belonging. His vast knowledge of the local sea life and the history of objects which adorned the seafloor was impressive. Her shyness vanished as quickly as did Proteus's warning to Glenn to "Be careful!"

As awesome and wondrous as were the discoveries Glenn and Muriel made while exploring the ocean's hidden treasures, nothing compared to the intense feeling that were stirring inside them for each other. They teased each other. They played tricks on each other, and soon, their childlike laughter softened to the sweet murmurings of two people in love. Theirs was a love affair for the ages.

One day, Muriel and Glenn saw a cave with an odd-shaped opening. They immediately swam to it, intending to go exploring.

Diving near the cave was a puffin, the clown of the sea. Glenn looked at him and decided his name would be Argyle, an Irishman, from the land of the Gaels.

Muriel was amazed that the colorful little creature came close to Glenn as though they were old friends. She felt her heart open wide as she watched Glenn and the bird interact.

"Glenn," she blurted out, "I love you."

Argyle was quickly forgotten as Glenn turned to Muriel. "I love you, too. I want to spend the rest of my life with you."

All the oceans went quiet. Not a sound could be heard from above or below the waters as Glenn took Muriel in his arms and kissed her with a depth of emotion that expressed his love and desire for her. He stroked her hair and cheeks tenderly.

The puffin attempted to poke his beak between them, and Glenn and Muriel laughed at his antics. Glenn, recognizing

Argyle's devotion to him, asked if he would be his best man. The feathered intruder cawed loudly, acknowledging his consent.

Suddenly, Argyle dove in the water and entered the cave. He quickly returned with something shiny in his mouth. Glenn held out his hand and the puffin dropped his gift into it. A gold ring set with sweet seed pearls and a beautiful emerald glimmered in the sunlight. The grooves in the gold looked like waves lapping over each other. Muriel gasped in shock and delight.

Glenn slipped the ring on Muriel's finger. There was a barely perceptible movement as the ring tightened just enough not to come lose. In that moment, a bond was formed that would never be broken – a bond between a man and woman who had found their soulmate. Glenn and Muriel stared into each other's eyes until the grunt of their puffin friend brought them back to reality.

As the star-crossed lovers beamed at each other as they swam back to the Valley and Wading River, it was if all of nature had gotten a telegram about the happy event that just happened. As they left their newly found love nest, sea seals were exuberantly clapping and honking at them. As they navigated off the Blanket Islands, a pod of dolphins surrounded them with clicks of glee and a once in a lifetime performance.

No sooner had the dolphins departed them than a hump backed whale decided it would be their sentry to the edge of the Valley. Glenn and Muriel felt as though Mother Nature herself was giving them a blessing.

As they approached The Valley, Glenn stopped suddenly, looked at Muriel in a solemn way and stated he had made a grave mistake, he would need the ring back. She looked at him for a minute not knowing who said this.

When it registered in her mind as to who said it and what was said, her soul was crushed. Then Glenn realized he had made two mistakes but this time explained. He could not ask for her hand till he spoke to her father, he was a Merman of principal and courtesy. There was peace in the Valley again.

Side by side, they swam to a tranquil part of the Valley where Irwyn and Mirasol had made a home for their family. Glenn approached Muriel's father and with great respect asked if he could speak privately with him. There was a special timbre in his voice - a quality of nervousness which Irwyn immediately recognized.

Being a good husband, Irwyn said that he would gladly speak with Glenn but asked that his wife be included in the conversation. Glenn apologized for this thoughtlessness in not thinking to include her.

Realizing that this would be the most important conversation of his life, Glenn choose his words carefully. He cleared his throat and spoke from his heart, "Irwyn and Mirasol, I am here to ask that you entrust me with the most sacred gift given to you by the Great Creator - Muriel. Your daughter has become my world. With your blessing, it is my intention to love and protect her for the rest of my life as my wife."

Irwyn and Mirasol looked at each other knowingly. They were not surprised as they had watched their daughter's feelings for Glenn grow from like to love. They had talked about her future as a woman and a wife.

What Muriel's parents were surprised by were the emotions that engulfed them. They had always felt love and pride for their daughter. Now, they felt equal affection for the Merman who had captured their daughter's heart.

It was Mirasol who was the first to answer. "Glenn, you come here today to ask Irwyn and me for permission to continue a life story which he and I started years ago. I have observed you and all you do in this Valley. My observations have convinced me that you are the only Merman who is worthy of writing those stories." Mirasol pulled Glenn close and embraced him. "Welcome to our family."

Irwyn added, "Glenn, my beautiful and sage wife has spoken for both of us."

He shook Glen's hand and the handshake turned into a group

hug with Mirasol and Muriel joining in. Glenn slipped the ring on Muriel's finger and promised not to ask for it back.

The newly pledged couple told the tale of the sea cave, Argyle, and the special escort that had followed them home. It was now time to tell Proteus and Salacia.

The newly affianced couple headed towards Glenn's familial home. Salacia saw them approaching from a distance. She knew her son very well, and she knew the news he was about to give them, "Proteus, come stand by my side, please." Her husband was intrigued by her request, but when he saw Glenn and Muriel swimming toward them, his question was answered.

Proteus had never seen his son so confident and happy. Love looked good on Glenn, and Proteus was thrilled for him. He reached for Salacia's hand and squeezed it affectionately. Glenn's parents looked at each and silently decided to play dumb so as not to steal their son's thunder.

The two couples greeted each other warmly. Salacia inquired about the surprise visit. Glenn cleared his throat, preparing to tell his parents the most important news of his life. He started, "Mother, Father, you have always been the most important people in my life and my regard for the two of you is boundless. I want to tell you that I have asked Muriel to be my bride."

Proteus and Salacia feigned shock. They clapped their hands in excitement and showered the couple with words of love and wishes for their continued happiness. Glenn told them the story of the sea cave and all that had happened on their way home. Both Proteus and Salacia were amused and impressed by Glenn's relationship with so many living creatures.

When the couple's engagement was formally announced, everyone in the Valley celebrated. A party was planned but not one of grand scale. Rather, the union of Glenn and Muriel was acknowledged with class and grace. The ceremony was to be a heartfelt rejoicing of two families and the community, all of whom were made to feel richer for sharing the undeniable joy that the happy couple had found in each other.

CHAPTER THREE

*"If I had a flower for every time I thought of you... I could walk
through my garden forever"*
~ Alfred Lord Tennyson ~

Glenn had decided they would spend their first night as husband and wife at the sea cave. The day before the wedding he snuck off to their special place. Glenn made long ropes of seaweed and he brought a larger fishing net he had found in his travels. There was a square part of a thatched roof that Glenn had seen on the beach nearby and he managed to get in the cave with the help of his newly made roping and the netting. It will make a nice bed he thought. He had taken some medium sized glass orbs and some wooden oars from a shipwreck. He secured the orbs in intervals along the roping. He then attached the oars upright to the four corners of the bed. As he was trying to figure out how to get the roping around the oars and the netting on top, Argyle appeared.

"Argyle, my old friend," Glenn shouted.

Argyle bowed, acknowledging that he knew his help was needed. He flew into the air, took a corner of the net and placed it in the oar. He did the same thing three more times with each corner of the fish net, until it made a canopy for the bed. He then went to work, grabbing the end of the sea weed roping from Glenn's hands. Soon, a beautifully woven canopy was hanging over the bed.

Glenn knew that on this night there would be a full moon, and he knew that the moonlight through the orbs would be magical.

"Perfect... just perfect, Argyle. I cannot thank you enough for your assistance. Please remember, our wedding is tomorrow and we would be honored to have you there."

Argyle bowed and flew off. Glenn took one last look around the cave. He was pleased with what he had created. He wanted to linger longer, but the hour was getting late. The time had come to return to Wading River and prepare for the nuptials.

There was joy in the valley. Wading River had always been a place in the valley where peace and tranquility could be found, but this day the little hamlet found a smile on everyone's face. The beams of sunlight from the world above went a little farther and a little wider.

As Irwyn and Mirasol prepared to take their daughter to the ledge where the ceremony would be performed, they realized this would be the last time their little family would consist of just the three of them. Muriel looked over to them and sensed what they were feeling.

"Mother, Father, I want you to know how much gratitude I have in my heart for you. It is because of all you have taught me that I am confidently becoming Glenn's wife today. I cannot remember a time when you have not been with me. Please know it does not end now. Today, I become Glenn's wife, but I will always be Irwyn's and Mirasol's daughter."

The parents grabbed their daughter's hands and held them tightly.

Mirasol said, "Muriel, you have given us many, many moons of happiness. We know your place is with Glenn and we look forward to seeing you become his wife. Then we will be able to welcome him as a son."

Irwyn spoke through tears, "From the time you came into this world, you have made your mother and I jubilant, but, today, you have topped yourself. You have not only become a Merwoman of intellect and genuineness, but you have also found your soulmate. By marrying this fine young Merman, you are making our family something grander than we ever imagined. We are not only proud of you, we thank you." Muriel then gave each of her parents a hug. It was time for them to go to the much-awaited event

The landing that was selected for the nuptials not far from where either the bride or groom lived. It was a part of the scenery in the community that they had passed many times without thought. The realization that it would be a perfect spot for them to exchange vows came on a day when they young couple saw how at a certain time of day the rays from the sun above broke into the depths of the sea and made it have the feel of an altar. It would be a perfect place for them to pledge their lives to each other.

As Irwyn, Mirasol and Muriel slowly made their way to the ceremonial site where Glenn and the elder were waiting, they were affectionately greeted by all of their neighbors. The landing was a brilliant spot in the underwater world that day. The sun radiated through the water and sparkled upon a bed of sea glass collected by all the Merfolk of Wading River - a bed of sea glass of umpteen colors and varying shapes. The beams of light gave the aura of a stain glass window.

Glenn saw his bride and was struck silent. Muriel, wearing her hair long and flowing, was more beautiful than Glenn had ever seen her. On her head was the same crown of jewels that her mother had worn on her wedding day. Her bouquet was made of treasures of the sea.

Smiling warmly, Muriel swam to Glenn's side.

The chief elder, Nereo, who was performing the ceremony, was obviously bewitched by the couple standing before him. He glanced around at the circle of Merfolk who were there to witness this event, giving a warm and knowing look to each and every one of them. The seas seemed to bask in this moment.

Since the Merfolk believed in an Almighty Creator, Nereo started the ceremony by giving profound thanks. He thanked Glenn & Muriel for letting the Merfolk of the Valley participate in this, the most glorious day in their lives.

He reminded those gathered that their bodies were half human and half water, a combination which gave them strength and understanding of two vastly different worlds. The humans living on the nearby land had some wonderful traditions that Merfolk could bring into their own lives should Muriel and Glenn ever choose to discover the world above the water.

Nereo told the story of an Irish fisherman who had felt a tremendous love in his heart for his wife. He wanted to present her with a wedding band that matched his feelings. He searched until he found a gold ring into which he carved two hands clasping a heart and a crown.

The crown stood for loyalty, the heart for love and the hands friendship. These qualities, the fisherman believed, were the basis for the strong relationship he shared with his beloved. He felt he and his wife were made stronger by sharing these qualities with each other.

The chief elder explained that a solid marital relationship begins with friendship. It grows stronger as a personal relationship is formed and continues to grow as a familial relationship and a community relationship are added.

At the conclusion of the story, Nereo asked the couple to hold hands. He asked the Merfolk in attendance to do the same. Reaching his arms out to the crowd, he said, "Look at how all the life arounds us thrives when we have a friend. When you have loyalty, you have a friend who is always there. Just as a husband and wife, parents to child, neighbor to neighbor. Look at what love does. For a couple, it has the power to create a future, a life that two make one. When we love our neighbor, it turns a community of many into one."

Nereo spoke directly to Glenn and Muriel, "My young friends, we will now witness the two of you pledge your life to each other in a relationship that was formed through friendship and will forever be bound by your love for each other. Your loyalty will transform days into years and years into decades."

He then asked Glenn, "Do you, Glenn, take this Merwoman to be your wife?"

"Yes," Glenn replied. "Forever and always."

Nereo looked at the bride and asked her, "Muriel, do you take this Merman to be you husband?"

"Yes. Forever and always."

Nereo asked Glenn if he had a token to give to Muriel. Glenn took out the ring that Argyle had given him. Nereo instructed Glenn to place the ring on his beloved's finger.

Glenn repeated, "Forever and always."

Nereo pronounced them Merman and Merwife and instructed them to seal the pledge with a kiss. They enthusiastically did as they were told.

Just then a band of bubbles surrounded the couple. Looking down, they saw a circle of seahorses breathing air bubbles that floated upward in the water.

They felt a current reaching them from the waters above, the current being caused by a pod of dolphins spinning in celebration.

Then, Glenn and Muriel caught sight of a brilliant red head moving quickly toward them. Argyle, diving to a depth of 200 feet, offered his congratulations before quickly heading back to the surface.

Their day could not have been more perfect.

The newlyweds departed for their honeymoon suite. As they were swimming away from the wedding celebration, they noticed two rows of lion-maned jellyfish lined up on either side of them as if to make an aisle. The now husband and wife were touched by the gesture.

CHAPTER FOUR

"Love doesn't make the world go round: love is what makes the ride worthwhile."
~ Elizabeth Barrett Browning ~

When they arrived at their special place and Muriel saw the room that Glenn and Argyle had created, she felt as though she was in a fairytale. As she looked around, she was overwhelmed by her husband's resourcefulness, ingenuity and, most especially, his ability to get Argyle to help him.

Filled with love, she swam into Glenn's arms and they embraced. The kind and gentle love they felt in their souls for each other came through in their bodies. As Glen had hoped, the moon did not disappoint; its fullness and brightness making their first night together more dazzling.

Glenn and Muriel found a place to call their own in Wading River near both their parents. They were deeply in love, and their home reflected their innate sense of caring. Life was their oyster.

Soon after the wedding, Muriel became pregnant. The news

that she was with child was met with exuberance by Glenn, his parents and in-laws and the entire community. The pride felt by the soon-to-be grandparents was nothing when compared to the happiness that filled the hearts of the young couple. Their child would be both their heart and their soul.

Mirasol was a constant calming presence in the final days of the pregnancy, helping Muriel with a myriad of tasks and advising her to rest as much as possible. This allowed Glenn time to explore the sea bottom for something special to give his child. The soon-to-be father found an enormous pear whelk and, instantly, realized the shell would make a perfect nest for their child.

He looked it over thoroughly and decided to make some needed alterations. He headed to the section of the valley where the community tools were kept. Taking an awl from one of the nearby shipwrecks, he made small holes on either end of the shell. He then took canvas from a schooner and made a sling into which the shell would fit. The final touch was to sew thin but strong rope to the ends of the shell. The rope would secure the canvas, thereby holding the whelk in place.

Glenn decided to surprise Muriel by presenting the shell to her at the sea cave. He secreted the whelk in the cave and made a seaweed pillow for Muriel to rest on. Then, he rushed back home.

Muriel welcomed him with open arms. He asked if she felt well enough to go on a small adventure. She enthusiastically answered, "Yes!" while bombarding him with a million questions.

"It is a surprise," Glenn answered over and over again.

When they went through the channel near the Blasket Islands, Muriel knew their destination and became curious. Glenn felt such thrilling sensation inside. The thought of being a father in a short time made his chest swell with pride but discovering this secure little nest for their child gave him a feeling that he was protecting his child.

Before he knew it, they were at the sea cave. Muriel cooed how she could not wait until their baby was born, and they could spend a family day here.

Glenn stroked his beard with his fingers and mused, "Well, that could be difficult. Transporting a wee one must be done with care."

Muriel could not believe her ears. She thought this sea cave had as a strong emotional attachment for Glenn as it had for her. Glenn patted the sea weed pillow he had created for her to relax on, but she stared at him as if he was an unknown creature she was meeting for the first time. Even so, she did as he asked.

Just then a loud noise and a familiar object falling from the sky startled them. It was Argyle. Muriel did not know what to think.

Glenn greeted the puffin with a huge cheer. Argyle bowed to the young couple, a sign of friendship from the amicable bird. As Muriel watched the reunion unfold, she saw her husband slip away and quickly return with something she had never seen before in his hand.

"For you and the newest member of our family," Glenn said, presenting his wife with the pear whelk turned cradle.

Muriel recognized that her gift was a canvas sling of some kind. She studied it and was amazed to find that the sling held the largest and most perfect pear whelk she had ever seen.

Glenn saw how Muriel looked at the sling and knew that his gift had been a success. Muriel carefully placed the sling on the ground and turned to give Glenn a hug. While still embracing, they heard a noise coming from the shell. Argyle stood next to it.

Glenn grabbed the whelk, fearing something that could harm his family had crawled inside. Instead, he found pearls hanging from the spire and down into the canal of the shell. The pearls were strung in a manner that would allow them to convert from three little stands to one larger strand. The pearls were like none that Muriel or Glenn had never seen before. The young couple looked on in amazement.

"Argyle, my old friend," Glenn said. "You have hidden talents. I did not know you were a gemologist? These pearls are the perfect gift for a baby girl!

Argyle bowed in acknowledgment of his gift's acceptance.

Glenn suggested that Argyle and Muriel join him in exploring the cave. The threesome was about to swim off when Muriel let out a sharp cry. "We must get home at once."

Glenn knew that fatherhood would soon be upon him. He rushed to his wife's side and helped her swim home.

The next day Muriel gave birth to their daughter. The entire family was overwhelmed by her presence. Muriel and Glenn had already decided that her name would be Rylee. Muriel placed Rylee in the pear whelk. It was a perfect fit.

Rylee was the talk of the valley. Mermen and Mermaids from every nook came to see their newest neighbor. She was showered with more strands of the finest pearls, rare coral shells, and combs made from whale bones by Mercraftsmen in the village. The combs were engraved with the initial R.

As the Merfolk from the hamlet came to meet Rylee, they deposited her gifts in her shell. The whelk provided a safe place for both the baby and her treasures.

CHAPTER FIVE

"A tragedy is a representation of an action that is whole and complete and of a certain magnitude. A whole is what has a beginning and middle and end."
~ Aristotle ~

*G*lenn and Muriel wanted Rylee to know of all the beauty that surrounded her. They often put her in her shell and took her to the nearby canyons and valleys. These trips of discovery were the happiest times for the little family.

One day, their excursion took them farther than they had planned on going. Glenn and Muriel realized that they were in the waters where they had met. They found an opening, a nook of sorts, which allowed them to easily reach the surface. From here, they could show Rylee the wonder of land.

No sooner had Glenn's head broken the surface of the water than Proteus' warning rushed into his thoughts. At the exact same moment, the sky grew black and the terrifying hiss of a sea serpent was echoed from behind him.

This creature was enormous... bigger than any Glenn had heard talked about in the village. Its gnashing front fangs were as long as Glenn was tall. The sound of the decades old barnacles and scales on its odious body filled the sea and the air with a sense of dread.

Knowing the destruction a sea serpent could cause would make any sea nymph or mortal fear for their future. For Glenn, the knowledge carried the burden of having to protect his wife and child. He put his arms around Muriel; she in turn moved to protect Rylee. Glenn knew their only hope for survival was to get into the crags of the cliff where, hopefully, the repugnant serpent could not fit into.

Holding Muriel and Rylee in his arms, Glenn propelled himself forward with the power in his strong tail. He had almost reached an opening in the rocks when he felt a sharp tearing in his back. The serpent's fang had ripped through him along the length of his spine.

As Glenn struggled to push Muriel and Rylee out of harm's way, the serpent's mouth engulfed all three of them at once and slammed them into the rocks. Glenn was overcome with pain. He felt the warmth of his blood as it gushed down his back.

A painful cry from the serpent brought him back to the moment, and he saw Muriel and Rylee being spat out onto the sands of the beach. He thought pain was distorting his eyesight; a trident appeared to be sticking out of one of the serpents" eyes. The creature was thrashing and hissing with rage.

The three prongs of the trident had penetrated deep an eye socket. Fluid was pouring from the wound. Glenn was transfixed by the power and ire of the serpent. He was frozen in place, almost forgetting to breathe. The wounded serpent convulsed in an effort to rid itself of the spear. Failing to do so, it retreated to deeper waters.

Glenn swam quickly, anxious to check on his family. He never knew relief and heartbreak could come so quickly, one upon the other. The pearl whelk had been a fortress for his baby girl and had protected her from harm. Muriel did not fare as well. The only part of her body that held form were her arms, which had cradled Rylee.

Glenn held Muriel as she tried to speak, concern for her husband and daughter on her lips. He whispered the necessary words of reassurance, but his heart was breaking. Suddenly, he heard a voice from behind him.

"Oh, my God."

A stranger was standing nearby. Glenn's first instinct was to lift Muriel and Rylee in his weakening arms and swim away, but the man, whom he realized was human, calmly told him to "Stay still. Do not move. I will help you."

The man came closer and examined the damage to Glenn's back. He explained to Glenn that he was seriously injured and must try to remain still. Glenn knew the man was right, but his primary concern was for his family.

The stranger turned to tend to Muriel's wounds. Unfortunately, the damage she sustained was internal. Glenn heard her struggling to breathe. He could see the color in her face draining away. Fear overtook him, paralyzing him. His mind rebelled. He could not lose Muriel. Their life together had just started. He looked up and saw the man holding Rylee, who was still in her shell. There were tears pouring from his eyes.

The stranger pulled Muriel and the baby to a section on the beach where they would be hidden from view. He did the same for Glenn. He then handed Glenn the secure pouch which had been made to hold Rylee. He removed a blanket from his knapsack and placed it over Glenn and Rylee to keep them warm.

With care, he propped Muriel's head up under a basket and covered her with a second blanket. He glanced over at Glenn holding his infant daughter and said, "I will try." Glenn knew the meaning of the stranger's words and he knew the man was sincere.

The human moved his hands in such a skilled and confident manner that Glenn knew healing others was his gift. Gently, he pulled Muriel's hair away from her face and, in that moment, he saw the full extent of her beauty. He stood breathless looking down at her.

The realization that he and only he could save this beautiful creature and that it must be done quickly, momentarily weakened his resolve. Upon examination, he saw that Muriel's airways were unobstructed although her breathing sounded labored. He knew without having to ask that Muriel had recently given birth. There were signs she shared with human females who had also given birth.

When the warmth of the blanket penetrated under her skin, Muriel's color began to improve, but it was not enough to sustain her. The stranger helped to move Glenn and Rylee closer to Muriel. "Talk to her. She can hear you. Encourage her to fight against the odds. She is showing signs of improvement," the stranger said.

For the first few seconds all Glenn could do was move his head back and forth from Muriel to Rylee. His love for the both of them was like fire in the night.

He whispered to his wife, "Muriel, you are my love. You are the mother of my child. I need you." The stranger heard Glenn's voice start to break. So did Muriel.

She opened her eyes and said in a whisper of a voice, "You, too, are my love. I love you as both my husband and the father of my child. I need you so very much, but I fear though we are out of time."

"No! No! No!" Glenn said as he shook his head, "The stranger will help you."

CHAPTER SIX

"We understand death only after it has placed it hands on someone we love."
~ Anne L De Stael ~

Suddenly, Glenn felt his body moving without conscious effort on his part. He looked down and saw that the lower part of his body was now human. With effort, he reached over to Muriel and lifted her blanket. She had changed as well. Hesitantly, he grabbed the shell that held his daughter and peered inside. She, too, had legs… tiny legs with tiny feet and toes.

Every Merman and Merwoman knew that when a Merfolk was out of the water for a lengthy period of time, they reverted to being human. Glenn had heard the stories often as a child, but this was his first time seeing it happen.

As he tried to grasp the significance of the change, he heard a soft moaning from Muriel. Her pain was a sad reminder of what had happened because he had failed to heed his father's warning. He seethed with anger for his own stupidity.

Finding strength, he did not know he had, he lifted Muriel in his arms. He told her of the depth of his love over and over again, but the longer he held her, the more he could feel her skin getting cold. His hands grew wet and he realized that the blanket was soaked with Muriel's blood.

Glenn raised his eyes in desperation to the stranger and pleaded, "Please, help us."

The stranger looked upon the family and saw that they had undergone a metamorphosis. Although a man of science, he believed he had witnessed a miracle. Their wounds, critical in nature, needed immediate attention, and he knew that he had a better chance of saving them in human form.

Muriel's condition was deteriorating rapidly. The stranger was helpless to do anything but make her comfortable. Glenn, in the meantime, had begun hemorrhaging from a deep gash in his back. The blood seemed to flow more quickly now that he was human.

To give himself room to work on both husband and wife, the stranger gently moved Glenn a short distance away. By the time he turned back to Muriel, she had passed on. He needed no words to relay the news to Glenn. The sadness on his face said it all.

Glenn crawled back to Muriel and, crying, he took her in his arms. He begged her unseeing, unhearing self. "Please do not leave me. Do not leave us. We have so much..." He could not continue as his tears consumed him.

Seeing the devastation on Glenn's face, the stranger's heart cracked. He knew there was an urgency for him to attend to Glenn's injury or he would suffer the same fate as his wife.

"I am sorry to disturb your sorrows. Please, I must attend to your injury."

The stranger pleaded as he gently pulled Glenn away from Muriel. He put Rylee, who was asleep in the shell, into Glenn's arms and then assessed his wound.

The laceration was deep but did not appear to have pierced any organs. Stitches were required but the stranger had no way of performing the task as he had no instruments with him. His face registered his struggle to find a solution.

When the man, who was slowly becoming less of a stranger and more of a savior, saw Glenn's eyes dart to the sky, he followed the direction of his stare. A dark figure was careening towards them. Argyle, the puffin, dropped a fishing hook with a piece of line attached.

The man was stunned and when he heard the Merman speak the bird's name, he was even more amazed. The puffin had brought what was needed to save the injured man's life.

The stranger turned savior took the shell containing Rylee away from Glenn and put it in a safe place on the beach. He told Glenn to brace himself, warning that he could help him but that there would be a tremendous amount of pain. Taking a deep breath, he pierced Glenn's body with the hook. Glenn cried out, then fainted. The man sutured the wound with deft movements.

At the water's edge, the stranger gathered long strands of seaweed. He wrapped the seaweed tightly around the wound area. Once the seaweed bandage was secured, the man carried Glenn to the water's edge, where the salt water and the nutrients from the seaweed would help keep away an infection.

As Glenn, who was still unconscious, rested the stranger went to check on Rylee. When he returned to Glenn, he was again stunned by what he was seeing. As the water lapped against Glenn's legs, they gradually became a long, beautiful tail... a fin. The stranger placed Rylee, still in her shell, on the ground.

Argyle could be heard crying as he stood guard over Muriel's body. The puffin cawed, seemingly to call to the stranger. The stranger went to where Muriel was laying. He picked her up and carried her to where Glenn was resting at the water's edge. Then, he placed Rylee between her parents.

The tragedy of the day was overpowering his resolve to stay strong. Tears poured down his face. His sobs matched those of Argyle, who was crying as he kept watch over his friends.

CHAPTER SEVEN

"It's always something to know you've done the most you could. But, don"t leave off hoping, or it's of no use doing anything. Hope. Hope to the last!"
~ Charles Dickens ~

he stranger composed himself and picked up the whelk containing the baby. He talked to her, telling her how sorry he was, as he was walked along the beach. He took time to examine the shell that cradled the little girl. Never had he seen a shell this large. The way in which it was fitted into the canvas showed ingenuity. Whomever had come up with the concept of using a shell for a baby carrier was a genius. The man found himself rocking the little girl, lulling her to sleep to the rhythmic sound of the waves.

As the stranger sat on the beach with the baby in his arms, Irwyn and Proteus reached the place which Proteus had cautioned Glenn to avoid. Word had spread through the Valley that a sea serpent had been sighted in the area.

Proteus thought back over his conversation with his son. He feared his warning had not been heeded. He could not silence the alarms sounding in his head and, not wanting to alarm Salacia, he told her he had an errand to run. He was on his way to check on his Glenn, Muriel and Rylee when he met Irwyn, who was also concerned for the couple and their child.

The two fathers shared feelings of unease for their children and granddaughter. Together, they went in search of them. As they got closer to the coast, they saw two figures in the surf and knew immediately it was their children. They could not swim to them fast enough, and when they finally reached them, they were stunned.

Glenn was alive but weak. He was unconscious, his breathing shallow. No words were needed to tell them that Muriel had passed. Irwyn knelt beside his daughter and took her hand in his own. She was cold. He began to cry.

Proteus had one hand on his son's chest and the other on his friend's shoulder. He looked for the baby and, not seeing her, cried out her name. "Rylee!" Scanning the area and seeing nothing, he lamented to Irwyn, "I do not see our granddaughter. I fear the worst."

The two men were frantically looking about when they saw a human in the distance. Panic filled their hearts. Each man grabbed his own child and hurried back into the water. As they swam away, two dolphins approached, a fishing net pulled taunt between them.

Irwyn and Proteus placed their children on the net. They dolphins carefully carried Glenn and Muriel back to Wading River. The fathers stayed close behind, their tears absorbed by the ocean waters.

Somehow, the dolphins knew that Nautica, the healing elder, lived along the river. Neighbors saw the dolphins approaching and rushed to tell Salacia and Mirasol. Irwyn and Proteus took control of the netting as they neared Nautica's home.

Seeing the bodies on the netting, Nautica realized that Glenn needed immediate care. She began unwrapping the seaweed and saw the sutures. Nautica knew that another learned healer had saved Glenn's life. She assured the gathered crowd that Glenn would survive but that his recovery would be long and arduous.

"The healing waters of the river are best for him now."

Together, Irwyn, Proteus and the assembled Merfolk helped to move him to a secure pocket where he would not be disturbed.

Salacia and Mirasol arrived and, seeing their children, collapsed into their husbands' arms. Salacia wanted to touch her son.

Mirasol extended a quivering hand to stroke her daughter's cheek. "What happened?!", she cried.

"The sea serpent," answered Irwyn through tears.

As the shock wore off, the two grandmothers asked, "Where is our granddaughter? We must find Rylee."

Their husbands agreed and although exhausted they and a small group of merfriends swam back to where they had found Glenn and Muriel... the place where they had seen the human stranger.

CHAPTER EIGHT

"Everyone you meet knows something you don"t know but need to know. Learn from them."
~ C. G. Jung ~

*D*r. Pradraig Knez loved the sea. He also respected and feared the sea. To live on an island as beautiful as Ireland was most definitely one of the graces God had given him. He had also been graced by the gift of survival. His thoughts often centered around the reasons that had brought him to Ireland.

Pradraig Knez was the son of Stjephan and Vesna Knez of Solin, Croatia. Solin is a small town in the southern Dalmatia. It is a city that goes back to the time of the Romans when it was ruled by the emperor Diocletian. Solin is a beautiful city with waterfalls, a river and the Klis Fortress.

Stjephan and Vesna Knez had met twenty years earlier in the town of Primosten, where Vesna had grown up. Stjephan, with his dark hair and olive skin, was never without female companionship.

He worked for a private shipbuilding company in Trieste, Italy. His dream was to open his own firm.

Stjephan was well-informed on expected changes in the maritime industry. He knew the coming years would give birth to men of vision and ingenuity. He knew he was such a man, and he wanted to share his creations with the world. Once he met the Mediterranean beauty Vesna, he knew he wanted her to be a part of his future.

After five years of hard work, Stjephan achieved two goals in one year. First was the success of his company and second was his marriage to Vesna. His business prospered and his marriage filled him with more happiness than he ever imagined possible.

While the shipbuilding company doubled in size, his private life remained a family of two — just Stjephan and Vesna. The couple longed to have a child. Stjephan knew that for six months Vesna had been walking to St. Mary's Church on Our Lady's Islet.

Vesna had always been religious, but Stjephan knew her reason was much more personal. Both he and Vesna had heard that taking a sip of water from the well near the church could cure infertility.

Stjephan never let Vesna know that he was aware of why she went to church so often. Six months after taking her first sip from the well, she informed him that they would be parents. Never had Stjephan experienced such happiness. When Pradraig when born, he was beyond himself with joy.

The young parents took their baby on nightly walks. They always took the path that led to the church. Never did they fail to stop and give thanks for the blessing that was their son.

Stjephan and Vesna found raising Prad to be a most rewarding experience. They loved parenting. They were financially secure and, when needed, they had help from Stephan's parents, who lived nearby. Vesna missed her family and the quaintness of Primosten, but Solin had become her home. She felt blessed that she and Stjephan were able to raise Prad in the seaside town.

As Prad grew to be a toddler, he became friends with a little girl named Tatiana. As the years passed, that friendship became the safety net that kept them strong whenever adversity struck. Watching the two children discover the wonders of the world around them was amazing Vesna and Stjephan.

When Prad was a young man, his family decided to take an extended trip to the United States. Stjephan's company was now owned by one of the most revered boat building enterprises on the Adriatic Coast. One of the reasons for the trip was a visit with Stjephan's brother, who was 15 years his junior. He adored his younger sibling and had named Prad in his honor. Pradraig was also the name of Stjephan's father, a daring sea captain who had traveled the globe.

Uncle Pradraig lived in London. He had moved to England many years before to study law at Oxford. When he finished his studies and officially became a barrister, he informed his family of his intention to remain in London. He had fallen in love with the city on the Thames and enjoyed the lifestyle it afforded him. Uncle Prad would write letters to Stjephan filled with tales of his fascinating life, including all the places he traveled.

It was the letter detailing his trip to the American colonies that Stjephan could not forget. After reading about his brother's exploits, Stjephan took the letters to his parents' house so they, too, could live vicariously through their other son's adventures. Pradraig senior was amazed at how quickly the colonies were changing.

Stjephan dreamed of the cities his brother described in his letters... cities with harbors big enough for sailing ships from the four corners of the earth. He felt obligated to take his family to see these places which were so different from anywhere they had been.

Stjephan talked with Vesna for hours, explaining this yearning that had possessed him. While Croatia was in their blood, both Stjephan and Vesna wanted Pradraig to experience all life had to offer. Though only twelve, their son excelled in school. He was naturally gifted in the musical arts and played the piano by ear. Prad spoke and wrote in five languages: Croatian, Latin, German,

French and Italian. Academics came so easily to him, his tutors often teased that he should be teaching them.

Stjephan began making arrangements for their journey. First on their itinerary was a stop in London to spend time with Uncle Prad. While there, Stjephan would conduct business in the United Kingdom. Then, they would set sail to see the land called America.

Young Prad had preparations to make as well. He had raised two dalmatians named Jupiter and Juno from the time they were born. The dogs were his constant companions, and he needed to find the right person to look after them. The only person he trusted was Tatiana. She readily agreed because having Jupiter and Juno with her would alleviate some of the sadness she felt about Prad's departure.

CHAPTER NINE

"Be slow to fall into friendship; but when thou art in, continue firm and constant."

~ Socrates ~

ondon was exhilarating for young Prad. At the time, it was the largest city in the world... the capital of an empire where the sun never set.

Solin seemed languorous compared to London, but whenever Prad saw carriages carrying the British noble class, he thought of home with its parks, olive groves, orchards and flowering shrubs. The wealthy in Solin traveled with their dogs for protection, just as did the English. The Croatian dog of choice was a dalmatian.

Uncle Pradraig arranged for his brother, sister-in-law and nephew to be shown all the best London had to offer. They toured Buckingham Palace, Simpson's in the Strand and the Criterion Theatre. Prad made notes in a small book he kept in his pocket. He wanted to share this adventure with Tatiana when he returned to Solin.

Uncle Prad had changed during his time in England. Due to his desire to fit in with London's elite, he had anglicized his name. He was now known as Patrick Kane.

Uncle Patrick, as he asked to be called, was a man of endless resources. He was one of the most sought after barristers in one of the world's largest cities. No one who knew him was surprised by his prowess in the courtroom. He was not only strikingly good looking, he was multi-lingual and possessed a confident air that opened many doors for him. On day one of the Knez family's arrival, Uncle Patrick began teaching his nephew the King's English, which young Prad mastered quickly. Soon, he would sound as if he was British by birth.

Stjephan took time away from the family to visit old school chums and colleagues in the maritime industry. He sometimes took young Prad with him. Prad loved his time with his father. Like a sponge, he absorbed his father's passion for shipbuilding. He enjoyed learning all he could at his father's side.

Stjephan was a wise man. He wanted Prad to enjoy the leisurely side of this trip. Education was important but so was having fun. One day, the family visited the London Zoo. Uncle Patrick had talked about the first public aquarium in the world and the Knez family was eager to see it. Prad had always had an interest in nature, but the zoo and the aquarium proved to be beyond his wildest dreams.

The visit to the zoological garden brought to life many of the animals his grandfather had spoken of seeing during his travels abroad. Young Prad's respect for his grandfather grew by leaps and bounds. He was proud to have been named for someone who had traveled the world and then come home to share his adventures with his family.

The array of majestic animals at the zoo left Prad speechless. The exhibits were so vast that there was only time to visit one venue each day. Visiting the aquarium would have to wait until every corner of the zoo had been explored.

Prad had seen paintings and heard stories of the sea while

accompanying his father on business. Now, he was able to see living specimens. Stjephan and Vesna were overjoyed that their son shared their love for sea life.

Prad was such an intelligent boy and everything seemed to come so easily for him. His parents worried that he would be easily bored, but Prad's enthusiasm bubbled like the bottomless tanks in the aquarium when he talked about all he had seen. He told his parents he could not wait to cross the ocean to America. He hoped to see new sea life in its natural environment.

London may have been the largest city in the world, but Belfast on Northern Ireland's eastern coast was the greatest for shipbuilding. One particular day, Stjephan had a meeting with Owen Boyle, a barrister for Harland and Wolff shipbuilders. The meeting had been arranged by Uncle Patrick, who was well-known in ship building circles.

Owen Boyle stood over six feet tall. His body was muscular with wide shoulders and a large head. He had a mane of reddish blonde hair that would make any woman jealous.

Stjephan and Owen made an instant connection. They were friends from the moment they shook hands. Unfortunately Owen announced that due to a family obligation, he would need to cut the meeting short.

With sincere apologies, he explained to Stjephan that he had promised to take his wife, daughter and his daughter's friend to the London Zoo. Stjephan smiled and offered young Prad as their personal guide. He explained that he, his wife and son had been to the zoo many times over the past few weeks and that Prad had the best route for seeing everything laid out in his mind.

When Stjephan relayed the news of another zoo trip to Vesna and explained the reason for going, young Prad was overjoyed. A trip to the zoo and new friends. There could be no better way to spend the day.

The two families met outside the entrance to the animal park. Stjephan and Owen made the introductions.

Owen's wife was Juliana. Their daughter was Mary. She had

been nicknamed Mazie while still an infant in her mother's arms. Her friend was Barbraella Sanders. The girls and Prad were all about the same age.

Since Prad was fluent in English and had even adopted a bit of a British accent, they all became quick friends. Prad led the little group along the path he had laid out; his parents continuing to be astonished by how much he knew about the animals living at the zoo.

The day was filled with fun and intrigue, and the excitement grew as the group entered the aquarium. As these two families' lives were woven into the sea, the sight of all the tanks filled with creatures which normally lived below the surface of the waters was enthralling. Prad described in detail the beautiful fish which swam in the tanks.

At the bottom of one of the salt water tanks was a miniature sunken ship. A Mermaid sat upon its bow. Barbraella, never one to be wooed by imagination, adamantly declared there were neither Mermaids nor sea monsters living in the ocean.

Prad related to the girls the stories his grandfather had told him. He said to Barbraella, "You are wrong. If my grandfather says they exist, they exist."

Barbraella turned her back with a loud harrumph, but Mazie, who had been hanging on to every word, believed Prad.

With the families getting along so well, the Boyles decided to invite the Knezes to their vacation home in Donegal, Ireland. It was decided that they would all travel to Belfast so Owen and Stjephan could conduct business. Afterward, there would be time to enjoy Donegal.

The Boyles, the Knezes and Barbraella took the the Flying Scotsman train from London to Edinburgh. Never had Stjephan and Prad been on such a fast moving transport. They found the ride exhilarating.

Upon arrival in Edinburgh, they were taken by a private carriage to Glasgow and after spending the night in in Scotland's largest city, the group went by private boat to Belfast.

CHAPTER TEN

"A friend is a priceless gem for the crown of life here and a
cherished star in memory forever."
~ *Cyrus S Nusbaum* ~

*B*elfast was a fascinating city with a long history and
Owen's knowledge of that history was vast. He shared
many stories with his guests. He explained how Belfast was once a
much smaller town, but even with a smaller population, it was
always busy. The farms and hills in Ireland supplied wool, hides,
grain, butter and meats which were shipped to England, Scotland
and France. Those countries reciprocated by sending delicacies
such as wine, fruit and cheese to Ireland. In the late 1600s,
Belfast's population grew mostly due to the arrival of French
Protestants who were fleeing religious persecution. Belfast
welcomed them.

These new immigrants brought the art of linen weaving with
them. Small town Belfast grew into a prosperous city but with the
growth came sickness. Rats arrived on every ship that docked at

the port. With more rats than people, the plague spread quickly. While Belfast had become world famous for linen, it was also becoming known for the deadly outbreaks of typhus and cholera that took the lives of its residents.

Owen Boyle had been personally hired by Edward Harland. As co-owner of Harland and Wolff, Edward's decisions were law. Harland and Wolff built ships for Cunard's White Star Line.

Owen was a hard worker; his professionalism raised him above other employees and he spent a great deal of time in London on company business. It was during one of his business trips that he met Patrick Kane, who greatly impressed Owen. On their first meeting, Owen predicted that Patrick (Prad Knez) was on his way to becoming a judge.

Owen and Juliana loved Belfast, but the city's unfortunate distinction as a dangerous place to live or visit due to the clashes between the Catholic and Protestants made them feel uneasy. They wanted a safer place for Mazie to grow up. Both Owen and Juliana were originally from Donegal so they knew the area well. They decided to build a home in a place called Glenties, situated north-west of the Bluestack Mountains.

During the trip to and from London, Barbraella proved to be a spoiled brat. She was uncooperative whenever she did not get her way. The Boyles explained that she was the daughter of one of the barristers who represented Harland and Wolff on business matters. The girl's parents lived a bon vivant lifestyle and Barbraella was often left at home with servants. As Mazie and Barbraella were the same age and as Owen and Juliana felt sorry for her, they invited her to spend time with them in London.

Stjephan and Owen conducted their business quickly and the group set off for their final destination. Barbraella stayed in Belfast, as her parents had returned from their latest excursion in Europe. Prad enjoyed his time with both of the girls, but he found that Barbraella could be a little sharp at times, a trait he found unappealing. He made a mental note to himself that, if ever Mazie and Barbraella came to Croatia, he would allow them to interact with Jupiter and Juno, but he would only entrust the care of his beloved pets to Mazie.

As the two families neared the town of Glenties, the Bluestack Mountains came into sight. The range, comprised of bare, rounded hills which were characteristic to the remote wilderness associated with Donegal, caused the entire Knez family to gasp. In winter, the mountains were a russet color which took on a red flush when the sun shone.

"Welcome to our piece of heaven," Owen said with a laugh. He went on to explain that they were now in County Donegal and that Glenties in Gaelic was pronounced Na Gleannta, meaning the Glens.

Offering a bit of a geography lesson, Owen went on to explain that Glenties was situated at the meeting of two glens and two rivers – the Owenea and Stranaglough. "Those mountains that took your breath away are called the Bluestack Mountains. There is no better place for fishing and hunting than here in Glenties."

The Boyles' house backed up to the Owenea River. Plans had already been made for a picnic along the river's banks. The whinny of horses could be heard in the distance as Owen, who was a great admirer of the powerful animals, had a few beautiful steeds in his stable. Seeing the excitement on the Knez family's faces, he offered them access to his stables and the horses. "Feel free to go exploring. The horses are all well trained. Even a novice rider has nothing to fear."

When the travelers arrived at the house, they were greeted warmly by Bernadette Clyne, the Boyles' housekeeper. Mazie explained that Bernadette took care of everything; she knew everything there was to know about running the house.

"You must meet her, Prad," Mazie smiled mischievously. "She is your best ally or worst enemy. Do not make an enemy of Bernadette."

Bernadette proved to be a beautiful woman of about 40 years of age. She had rich auburn hair and emerald green eyes. Standing ramrod straight on the front porch, she studied the newly arrived guests.

When her eyes came to rest on Prad, she said, "Young man, let me look at you."

Prad moved closer and Bernadette took his hands in hers. She cupped his face and said with great seriousness, "Ireland will become another home to you, Pádraig. You are now one of her sons."

With a warm laugh, she directed them to the banks of the river where a table had been set with good Irish tea and warm food to fill their bellies. A snap of her fingers brought a houseman to carry the luggage. No one ever ignored an order when spoken by Bernadette.

What waited for the group was a welcomed surprise, especially in light of how long the trip had taken to complete. The sweet-smelling air was filled with the aromas of steeping tea, freshly baked scones, homemade jellies and other delicacies. No sooner did the guests take their seats than bounding from the house came the family pets – two large Irish wolfhounds named Zeus and Hera.

Mazie called to the dogs in an encouraging voice. "Zeus. Hera. Come meet our new friends."

Seeing how readily Zeus and Hera accepted their outstretched hands in a gesture of friendship, the Knez family knew they were in the right place. Once the dogs had finished with their greetings, everyone relaxed and prepared to enjoy the food Bernadette had prepared.

Juliana asked that they take a minute to give thanks and they all joined hands and bowed their heads. She prayed for the blessing of new friends and for the feast in front of them. She added a special request that the Knez family would be safe on their soon-to-be journey.

Watching Bernadette handle all the household duties, Vesna repeatedly said, "That woman is a treasure."

Whenever Owen and Mazie overheard these comments, they would nod vigorously in agreement. Mazie was of the belief that

Bernadette was magical, to which Owen would always reply, "Not magical. No. She is efficient."

Juliana laughed, listening to her husband's and daughter's comments. "I must warn you, Mazie and her father bicker constantly about the reason why Bernadette is such a wonder. I agree with both of them. Bernadette is a gift from the heavens."

Juliana went on to explain. "Owen and I had recently been married. We were visiting Father Patrick O'Donnell, who is now Bishop O'Donnell, in Raphoe. We were telling the Father of our future intentions of building a house in Glenties. Without a moment's hesitation, he pronounced, 'I have the perfect person for you.' From that point on, Bernadette was a part of our lives."

To prove Bernadette's importance, Owen motioned toward the river. "Look at our boathouse. Bernadette ordered all the materials and hired the men to design and build the structure. That has never been a woman's area of expertise, but Bernadette is not just any woman. She is amazing."

He further explained that every time he, Juliana and Mazie go away, Bernadette managed to complete another project.

"When I ask who helped her, she tells me help is given by a group of lads she has known for years. As I already said, she is amazing."

Half-jokingly, Stjephan and Vesna said they would be eager to see what Bernadette and her lads would accomplish by the morrow.

CHAPTER ELEVEN

"To live is the rarest thing in the world. Most people exist, that is all."
~ Oscar Wilde ~

$\mathcal{A}$t breakfast the next morning, Prad asked Bernadette how she learned all that she knew how to do. She answered that she relied on a neighboring couple for assistance. The husband helped with the house and grounds while the wife served as the children's tutor. Their names were Michael and Marion Dorman and they were very capable people.

Since everything Bernadette undertook to do was always a success, the Boyles' acquiesced to her suggestions. It was obvious that she brought only the best people to help at the Boyle Manor.

After breakfast, the adults decided to stroll about at the grounds while Prad and Mazie would spend the morning with Mrs. Dorman.

When the children entered the study, Mrs. Dorman greeted them by saying, "Dzień dobry."

Prad replied, "Cześć, fajnie jest poznać kogoś z Polski."

Mazie did not speak but her eyes held question marks of curiosity. Prad explained that Mrs. Dorman was Polish and that she had wished them "Good morning." He, in return had said, "Hello. It is nice to meet you."

Mrs. Dorman motioned for the children to sit down as she explained that she had moved from Warsaw to London when she was about their age. She met her husband in London and together they decided to move to Ireland. She was excited to learn that Prad spoke numerous languages and with Mazie's command of English, Gaelic and French, she expected the three of them to learn from one another.

While the children were getting acquainted with Mrs. Dorman, the adults visited the boathouse.

Michael Dorman was already hard at labor completing the aesthetic work that would give the building a distinctive flair. Stjephan marveled at the workmanship. Michael explained that while he had put in a great deal of work, it was Bernadette who deserved the credit.

"I arrive in the morning to find that 'her lads' have already gotten things done. They leave me unbelievably beautiful pieces of wood with which to work."

He further explained that he discussed everything that needed to be done with Bernadette and, lo and behold, within days he is able to complete a project.

Stjephan, who was surveying the boathouse with a keen eye, continued to offer compliments on its construction and design. The Boyles owned a few canoes, a currach and a coracle, which were stored inside. At the dock, a larger vessel was tied securely to the mooring. Made of wood, the ship was steam powered and outfitted for pleasure.

His curiosity peaked, Stjephan asked who was the vessel's

manufacturer and Owen told him, "Bernadette had some local lads do it. Grand! Is it not?"

Having attended university and having appriced to become a ship builder without ever seeing such exquisite workmanship, Stjephan was in awe. He noticed that the boat had been fitted to accommodate above average height people and those who were shorter than the norm.

Owen explained that his friend, Henry Kelsey, would often entertain his children on the boat. Bernadette knew this and had the boat built so the wee ones would be comfortable and learn boating safely. In passing, he mentioned that Henry ran the Bank of Ireland in Donegal.

Among Owen's favorite reminiscences was the story of how he and Henry had become friends. They met while both were students at Dublin University. Henry invited Owen to his family's home on the weekends, and the family welcomed him like a blood relative. During those weekends, Owen formed a close friendship with Henry's brothers, Blake and Christopher.

Over the summer months, Henry, Blake and Christopher would visit with the Boyle family in Donegal. Blake had been a skilled boater, but he tragically passed away in his early twenties. Christopher became an engineer. He lived in Dublin.

Owen's heart was in his voice when he said, "I have very warm feelings about these three men and, especially, their mother Elaine. It was quite a surprise when Henry took charge of the Donegal branch of The Bank of Ireland. He has helped many families in need, but that is not public information."

Stjephan asked how the name for the boat had been chosen, and Owen explained that he had not made the decision to name the boat for Blake Kelsey. Bernadette decided to do that after hearing the stories of how Owen and the Kelsey brothers became friends

Over dinner that evening, Owen informed Stjephan that arrangements had been made for them to play a round of golf at Ardara. Their tee time was 8:00 am. Special plans had been made for Vesna to visit with Bishop O'Donnell in Raphoe. She would be accompanied by Juliana, who wanted to present the Bishop with something she had bought while in London. Prad would go with Owen and Stjephan. The threesome would head south where a day of adventure would await them.

As dinner progressed, Vesna and Stjephan continuously praised the taste and quality of the meal. Juliana proudly explained that the spring salmon, grilse and sea trout were from the Owenea River and among the best available. Whenever she was in the United Kingdom, she was sure to purchase quality meats and seafood as well as various fruits and vegetables for Bernadette to serve the family and their guests.

Bernadette politely inquired if the Knez family was familiar with Donegal tweeds, the very best tailor-made clothing available anywhere in the world. Vesna's questioning eyes prompted Juliana to explain that Donegal Tweed had been woven locally for centuries.

While for some locals, the weaving of tweed was a steady occupation, for others – like the farmers and fisherman – it was a sideline that provided extra income.

"You cannot go on about your travels without first visiting John McGee at his store. McGee has a prime location in the Diamond, which is what we call the main square in Donegal Town. We will have an enjoyable afternoon there as there is much to see."

As the evening waned, Stjephan thanked Owen and Juliana profusely for sharing their beautiful home with him and his family. He extended an open invitation to the Boyles to come to Solin once they had returned from the States.

Owen enthusiastically replied, "I look forward to planning such a trip very soon."

Over a glass of spirits and a handshake, a friendship was secured that would last a lifetime.

Juliana then suggested the group go down by the river's edge. As they ambled past the boat house, they came upon a grotto.

A statue of the Blessed Mother stood protected in a cave built of granite boulders. The cave was adorned with Donegal wildflowers.

In front of the cave was a bench where believers could sit and meditate.

"What a beautiful statue of the Mother Mary," Vesna remarked as she grabbed Stjephan's hand.

"She is the Rosa Mystica," replied Juliana, directing Vesna's attention to the name chiseled in the base of the statue.

"I would like to impose a favor on you if I could Vesna? You are going to America. I have a sister, Mary Ellen, in New York... in Brooklyn to be exact. Can I ask that you please bring the statue on your trip and deliver it to her?"

"It would be our honor and pleasure," Vesna said, sincerity in her voice.

"To thank you, Owen, Mazie and I will have another statue shipped to your home in Croatia."

Juliana reached for Vesna's hands and together they said a prayer of gratitude.

Stjephan remarked to Owen that his house was located in a most beautiful and captivating place. He said that he, Vesna and Prad could never thank him enough for sharing his home and his family with them. Stjephan again extended an invitation to the Boyles to visit Solin whenever possible.

Owen replied, " I look forward to planning a trip there soon."

Bernadette was within earshot and wiped a tear from her eye.

CHAPTER TWELVE

"Some people look for a beautiful place. Others make a place beautiful."
~ Hazrat Inayat Khan ~

The next morning both families were treated to an early morning feast prepared by Bernadette. As they sat and talked about their upcoming day, they noticed that on the table were two tweed caps. Since the names of the owners of these caps were embroidered on the inside, it was obvious that one was for Stjephan and the other for Prad.

Prad quickly donned his hat and modeled it for all to see. Vesna gently reminded him that it was impolite to wear a cap at a dining table.

As each trio set out in different directions, the men tipped their caps to the ladies. The ladies coach was filled with basic necessities and decadent delights for the bishop. Hera traveled with the ladies. The men had a bountiful basket of sandwiches and libations. Zeus was their travel companion.

Vesna and Juliana looked forward to the ride up to Letterkenny, especially since Mazie was with them. Juliana and Mazie took turns explaining to Vesna the Boyle family's connection to Bishop Patrick O'Donnell.

Vesna learned that Patrick O'Donnell was born and raised in Kilraine, just near Glenties. He was very much the pride of the wee little town. On his father's side, the Bishop was a descendent of the O'Donnells of Tyrconnell, one of the two most domineering and famous clans of Donegal. On his mother's side, he was descended from the O'Neill dynasty, one of the most prominent families in Northern Ireland.

Patrick O'Donnell had received his secondary schooling in Letterkenny, the destination of the trio. Afterwards, he continued learning at the Catholic University in Dublin and Maynooth. He was ordained a priest in 1880, but being blessed with a brilliant mind, he was soon selected to hold a chair in dogmatic and moral theology at St. Patrick's College.

In 1885, Patrick was not only named a Dean, he was awarded his Doctorate. As if he had not done enough, in 1888 he was appointed Bishop of Raphoe, the youngest man ever to be appointed to that position.

Juliana beamed with pride telling of Bishop O'Donnell's success. The bizarre part was that Owen and Juliana could easily have changed places as Owen was telling the exact same story to Stjephan and Prad at the exact same moment.

The Boyles' coach arrived in Letterkenny after a trip that involved the giggling of a little girl, warm words of friendship between two ladies and deep sighs of appreciation from all three for the endless beauty Donegal had to offer. As the travelers stepped out of the coach, they stood in the shadow of two great things. One was a cathedral. The other was Bishop Patrick O'Donnell.

"Maidin mhaith na maidine. Gabhaim buíochas as do thuras sábháilte," said the Bishop warmly as he looked to the sky.

"Go raibh maith agat an tEaspag O'Donnell," answered Mazie.

The Bishop turned and addressed Vesna, "Excuse my poor manners, dear lady. I was simply saying in the native tongue of this grand country, 'Good morning' to all three of you and expressing my thanks for your safe arrival."

Turning to Mazie and smiling broadly, the Bishop said, "The future of our country, in the form of this young lady, thanked me in return."

Bishop O'Donnell praised Juliana for keeping Ireland's language alive by teaching her daughter to speak the Gaelic tongue. Juliana nodded in appreciation of his compliment. She immediately focused her eyes on the building behind him. Mazie and Vesna did the same.

The aspirations of the Cathedral of St. Eunan and St. Columba had begun in 1830. Finally, nearing completion, the Cathedral's majesty dominated the landscape. While it was Bishop O'Donnell who had commissioned the stunning Victorian neo-Gothic style building, it was the dream and hard work of many generations of clergy and lay people living in the town of Letterkenny, County Donegal, Ireland who had made the cathedral possible.

Professional craftsmen and laborers did the bulk of the heavy labor, but the extra special touches were added by the townspeople. The white sandstone that formed the base of the cathedral came from the village of Mountcharles in the south of Donegal County. The sandstone was shipped north along the coast via the Swilly River to Letterkenny. Town residents formed a bucket brigade which enabled the building material to move quickly from the shore to the construction site.

Bishop O'Donnell, seeing how impressed his visitors were with the structure before them said, "The reason the cathedral was originally started was to bring back memories of past good, wise and noble people and to put those qualities into the spirits of the present. St. Eunan's will honor every fallen shrine in Donegal by embedding a stone from each of those shrines in its construction. Inside the cathedral, there will be an altar or window or tablet dedicated to every patron saint from every parish in the diocese."

The Bishop liked to say that the cathedral was "... a building to gladden the hearts and ennoble the ideas of our downtrodden. It would remain for the ages not only a memorial, but a resurrection of the fallen shrines of Donegal."

Juliana suddenly realized that she had failed to introduce Vesna to the Bishop. In an effort to cover her embarrassment, she explained that the Knez family was visiting from the town of Solin in Croatia.

Bishop O'Donnell's eyes lit up. "Ah, Mrs. Knez, were you there 20 years ago when the Church of St. Mary's - Our Lady of the Islet came to life? I do believe I also heard of some recent archeological finds there."

Vesna, surprised by the Bishop's knowledge of her church, replied happily, "You are right on all accounts."

While the ladies and the Bishop spoke, the coachman who had driven Juliana, Vesna and Mazie to the cathedral stood patiently waiting by the carriage.

"Mrs. Boyle," Bishop O'Donnell inquired, "am I to assume that you are about to bestow many blessings upon me?"

"Now, Bishop, I was taught that one should never assume. However, in this instance you are correct. I have brought supplies for your schools. I am sure that St. Eunan's Presentation Brothers School and St. Columba's Convent National School will make good use of these items. I brought some homemade goodies as well... made by the loving hands of Bernadette Clyne."

The Bishop raised his hands in a blessing and the crates and boxes were unloaded with the help of the coachman. "Mrs. Boyle, your family's legendary generosity is a foil to the harshness of Mr. Boyle's Uncle Rod."

Juliana explained to Vesna that Uncle Rod was an absentee landlord. He was obsessed with greed. While some landlords displayed concern for their tenants, Uncle Rod threatened eviction, without notice, if tenants were delinquent in their payments. There were times when he evicted tenants for no reason at all. He just wanted them gone.

"Neither Owen nor I approve of him and, more often than not, we refuse to speak his name."

Juliana went on to explain that Bishop O'Donnell was a keen Nationalist. Not only was he involved in the day to day running of his diocese; he was also involved in the Plan of Campaign and Congested Districts Board, which gave aid to his parishioners and his fellow countrymen in their struggles against landlordism.

With an elegant bow and sweep of his arm, Bishop O'Donnell took the ladies on an abbreviated tour of the cathedral. Vesna was fascinated to learn the history of the church. The Bishop explained that the cathedral was built on the site of another church constructed in 1830.

Pointing toward Sentry Hill in the near distance, he explained that a sentry kept watch while priests celebrated Mass during the years of persecution. "At least, that is what tradition holds to be true."

Rodger's Burn, located less than a mile from the cathedral, had been the site of an old mass rock – a tangible link with the time of Penal Laws. A mass rock, Juliana explained, was a stone used as a Catholic mass altar in mid-17th century Ireland.

Bishop O'Donnell took pride in showing Juliana, Vesna and Mazie the Penal Cross, which held a special place in the cathedral and served as a reminder of the days when practicing the religious rites of Catholicism was prohibited. Such crosses were specially made to be easily hidden. Mazie's eyes grew bigger the more she looked around the cathedral.

In an awed little girl's voice, she asked Juliana, "Why was it necessary to hold mass in secret."

Juliana patted her daughter's arm affectionately and said, "That is a story for another day."

Once the tour was over, the little group adjoined to the parochial house to have lunch. Relaxing over their meal, Juliana and the Bishop had time to catch up family and community news. Juliana, Owen and Patrick O'Donnell knew each other well. They were long-time friends, having gone to school together when they were young children.

Seizing on a pause in their conversation, Juliana thanked Patrick for bringing Bernadette into their lives. Her words made him smile with delight and he expressed his happiness that they were all doing well.

With a bit of hesitation, he explained that he might have to snatch Bernadette away from them for a short time. Her services would be needed during the dedication and opening of the church as people would be coming from as far away as Australia and New Zealand. Juliana promised to inform Bernadette of the Bishop's request.

As their time together drew to an end, the Bishop suggested that the driver take them for a drive past River Swilly. There they would be able to grasp the devotion and fortitude of the townsfolk who carried the sandstone for the construction of the cathedral. They agreed that the detour would be well worth the time.

Vesna promised Bishop O"Donnell she would give the priests from her home parish his regards. Prayers of safety and wellness were offered before the ladies boarded their coach. Far into the distance, they were still waving goodbye to the man they all held in high esteem.

The land around River Swilly was beautiful, lush and green with trees in abundance and cows munching on their vegetarian lunch. A berm separated the road from the water, and Mazie asked if she could explore the riverbank. Juliana gave her consent and her daughter bounded out of the carriage with all the enthusiasm of a curious twelve-year-old. She headed straight to the water.

Vesna brushed her hair back, and in doing so, her beautiful pearl ring was in evidence. Juliana commented on the ring which allowed Vesna to say that it was the first gift Stjephan had given her. She explained that Stjephan's father had found the ring in a shop in Australia. He gave it to his son with the strict instruction to give it to the girl of his dreams.

"The first Christmas we were courting, Stjephan gave the ring to me as a gift. He told me of his father's wish. He also made me promises for our lifetime together, which he has more than kept and, in fact, superseded. I look forward to the day I can give the ring to Prad so he can give it to the woman of his dreams." Vesna paused and then said with a laugh, "But not too soon."

Juliana and Vesna remained in the coach, reliving the past few hours with the Bishop and all they had seen and talked about. They did not see Mazie and Hera make their way to the water's edge or the hand waving at Mazie from a few feet off shore. Mazie enthusiastically waved back and took note that the girl waving to her was about her own age and had long blonde hair. Excitedly, Mazie motioned for the girl to come closer, but she dove down into the water, allowing what appeared to be a fish tail to protrude through the waves. Mazie had seen her first Mermaid!

CHAPTER THIRTEEN

"Life is partly what you make it and partly what it is made by the friends we choose."
~ Tennessee Williams ~

hile the ladies visited with the Bishop, Owen, Stjephan and Prad were happily on their way to Ardara Golf Club. Owen kept his travel mates entertained by talking about Bishop O'Donnell's remarkable accomplishments.

"The Bishop is the pride of all Donegal," Owen said, more than a wee bit of pride in his own voice.

Since neither Stjephan nor Prad had played golf, Owen patiently spent time explaining the rules of the game. He told them why the game was becoming important in Ireland, especially in their part of the country.

He chuckled when he said that the best way to describe golf's hold on the country was a quote he had read in the popular newspaper, *The Scotsman.* "... until recent times, a chapter on Irish golf would have been as substantial as that on snakes in Ireland." He went on to say that while currently there were but a handful of courses, many more were on the way.

The trip took the travelers past railroad tracks which Owen said were responsible for helping businesses in the area to grow. He expounded on how, in the few years the West Donegal Railway had been running, the hotels along the coast as well as nearby stores and eateries had seen an increase in profits. The railroad had attracted enterprising men to set up shop in Donegal, and the wealthy flocked to their doors.

With a hesitant smile, Owen admitted that he did not often take the train and he begged that his travel-mates not laugh at his reason. "When I travel by coach, I am able to share the beauty of the countryside with all living creatures. The horses and the dogs seem calmer and happier when they are able to commune with nature. I believe these animals, which we often take for granted, are much smarter than we realize."

When Stjephan and Prad quickly agreed, Owen continued to talk about how throughout history horses and dogs had worked beside man.

"Animals are responsible for much that has been accomplished."

He noted that Juliana and Mazie had a special fondness for cats, which they all held in high esteem for their intelligence.

Owen made mention of Flynn, the handsome cream-colored Connemara pony that was leading their coach. He explained that while Flynn was not as tall as some of the other horses in the stable, he had the heart and soul of a giant. He further explained that Sullivan, the black Welsh cob that was harnessed to the coach transporting Juliana, Vesna, and Mazie was native to Wales. Welsh cobs were usually smaller than the Connemara.

"Some land owners prefer bigger breeds, but these animals are as much a part of Ireland's history as are the people. Irish ponies tend to be smaller in stature but strong of will."

Owen continued to praise the beauty of God's canvas as the

coach made its way to the golf course. Everywhere they looked, there were green fields and clear blue seas. Stjephan and Prad could not help but be caught up in his enthusiasm for the gifts of nature. The trip was turning out to be a blessing in more ways than one.

The Nesbitt Arms Hotel, where the golf course was located, was nestled in a valley surrounded by spectacular scenery. Owen checked in while Stjephan and Prad enjoyed the view and thanked Flynn for getting them to their destination safely. Flynn nudged the pocket of Prad's blazer in response, which prompted Prad to feel for what held the horse's interest. Inside the pocket, he found carrots, put there no doubt by Bernadette

Prad was a little hesitant to feed Flynn, as the horse's mouth was moving quickly toward his hand. Stjephan instructed his son to put the carrots in his palm, flatten his hand and hold it out to Flynn. Prad laughed as Flynn's whiskers brushed against his skin. Zeus, not to be left out of the feeding, barked and Prad shared the carrots with him.

Owen cleared his throat as he returned from the hotel lobby. "Gentlemen, I am afraid that the hotel is busier than expected. They were forced to give our tee time to their registered guests. We can, however, play the last hole so you will, at least, have the thrill and the experience of playing golf."

"Not to worry, Owen," Stjephan said. "I will still be able to give my brother, Patrick, a report on what it is like to play golf in Ireland."

Once at the tee, father and son watched Owen intently as he placed a little ball atop a little peg. A few quick instructions on how to hold a club and how to position their bodies followed and, then, they were ready to play.

Owen went first and hit for par. Stjephan and Prad followed, scoring one under par. Prad wrote notes on his experience in the book he always carried in his pocket. He would share these with his uncle and Tatiana when next they met.

Shaking hands and congratulating each other on a stellar

performance, Owen pronounced that one man's bad luck was another man's good luck.

"Today, we have had a bit of both. Since we have time on our hands, why don't we spend it viewing the waterfalls? Agreed?"

CHAPTER FOURTEEN

"The world is big and I want to have a good look at it before it gets dark."
~ John Muir ~

lynn pulled the coach so close to the first waterfall that Owen, Stjephan and Prad could feel the mist from its pounding waters on their faces. This was Assaranca, considered to be one of the most beautiful waterfalls in County Donegal. Pronounced Eas a'Ranca in Gaelic, it was located in idyllic surroundings close to Maghera Beach.

Seeing the gushing waters, Stjephan and Prad stared in awe. There were beautiful waterfalls in Solin but none as forceful as Assaranca.

"Now you understand why I refer to this land as God's canvas." Owen swept his arm in a gesture that took in all their eyes could see. "Assaranca's waters never stop flowing on their way to the Atlantic Ocean."

With the beauty of Assaranca etched into their memories, they climbed back into the coach and Flynn began their journey again. The next stop would be Largy. Owen explained that they should not dawdle for the Secret Waterfall could only be seen at low tide or they would risk injury. The mention of a *secret waterfall* had Prad practically jumping out of his seat.

Soon, Owen called for Flynn to "Stop!" and Stjephan and Prad immediately understood why the waterfall had such an intriguing name. It could be heard but not seen. With Zeus acting as their guide, they began to climb the coastal rocks. Below, they heard Flynn whiney a note of caution.

After a few slips and slides and a near fall, the three intrepid climbers reached their destination. Entering the cave, the men stopped short and removed their caps out of respect for what their eyes beheld.

"Another of God's canvases," Owen said, pointing to the many brilliant colors heightened by the rays of the sun which reflected off the walls

While Stjephan and Prad would have gladly remained in the cave for hours, Owen reminded them of the incoming tide. With one last look at the *secret* that had been revealed to them, the men took their leave.

Zeus again went first, guiding them back down the slippery rocks. Suddenly, a gust of wind turned Prad's cap into a kite. It flew off his head and was carried across the rocks. Without thinking of the danger, Prad began to chase the cap, shouting back to his father and Owen that he feared Bernadette would scold him if he lost it.

Zeus barked and the caution in his voice caused Prad to stop, but it was too late. His feet slipped on the wet outcropping and he fell flat on his back, hitting his head on the rocks with a loud thud. Zeus barked again and Owen and Stjephan froze in horror as they watched Prad hit the ground in slow motion. He remained there motionless.

The dog moved first, rushing to Prad's side. He began licking Prad's face, which thankfully stirred the boy from his dazed state.

He raised his hand to Zeus' face in both gratitude and a need to make him stop licking.

As his dizziness cleared away, Prad heard his father calling to "... remain still. I am coming."

Owen, too, warned him not to move for fear he could fall again. The two men reached Prad's side and Owen assessed the situation. With the tide rising, they needed help. Flynn's now incessant whiney coming from below was the answer to their prayers.

Cautioning father and son to remain where they were, Owen made his way back to the carriage. He removed Flynn's reins and led him up the rugged terrain. Prad now had four rescuers to meet his needs. Zeus and Flynn worked together to get him back to level ground.

Prad used Zeus to stabilize himself as he stood up. Flynn remained absolutely still as Stjephan and Owen helped Prad to climb on his back. Slowly and cautiously, the caravan made their way back to safety. Stjephan, anxious for his son to be treated by a doctor, felt hours had passed rather than minutes.

Back in the coach, Prad wrapped his arms around Zeus' neck and gave him a kiss. He had done the same to Flynn before being helped down by Owen and his father. These animals had saved his life. He would never forget them.

Once Owen had checked the seriousness of Prad's injury, he harnessed Flynn to the coach. Prad was settled into the back, with Zeus offering himself as a warm pillow on which to lay his head.

The journey home was slow so as not to cause any bouncing that might cause Prad pain.

~

A similar scene was playing out on the shore of the River Swilly, where Juliana, Vesna, Mazie and Hera, Zeus' sister wolfhound, were resting.

Mazie and Hera had been playing, running from the water's edge to the carriage and back again. Suddenly, Hera came to a halt and began barking in an excited manner. At that same moment, Sullivan started to stomp her hooves. Hera jumped onto the carriage and stood next to the coachman, nudging him and lightly biting him on the arm. Juliana recognized the message in both animals' behavior. She instructed the coachman to take them home quickly.

Seeing that the coach carrying her husband and their guests had arrived home sooner than expected, Juliana knew something was wrong. Owen, Stejphan and Prad were nowhere to be seen, and Flynn was wearing his harness. Normally, Owen would have have unhitched the horse, taken him to the stable and tended to his needs before tending to his own. Hurrying into the house, the ladies saw Owen and Stjephan waiting nervously in the study.

"What has happened?" asked Juliana.

Owen explained the day's events. He comforted the ladies by saying that Bernadette was with Prad. She had asked that they leave her alone with the boy for a few minutes so she could clean his wound. A doctor was on the way.

CHAPTER FIFTEEN

"No act of kindness, no matter how small, is ever wasted."
~ Aesop ~

*W*ith the same tenderness his mother would have used to care for him, Bernadette tended to Prad. She told him that he had a bump the size of a "goose egg" on his head and that it could be a serious injury.

Prad, trying to lessen his pain with laughter, asked, "How big is a goose egg?'

"Big!" Bernadette answered, stifling the giggle that formed in her throat. "Goose eggs are almost five inches in length and, at least, seven inches around. This bump on your head is twice that size."

Prad reached his hand up to feel if the bump was really that large or if Bernadette was having fun at his expense. Before his hand was half way to his head, Bernadette pushed his fingers away.

"No touching!"

She assured him that she had sent for a doctor but, while they waited, she would like for one of her friends to exam his head. She told Prad that the friend was a special man who had healing powers. If Prad agreed, he would have to promise never to tell anyone... not anyone... of this man's visit. Prad sleepily nodded his assent.

"Aloysius, please come out."

Through half-closed eyes, Prad saw a small portion of the bedroom wall begin to open. From behind a bookcase, a man of no more than four foot tall entered the room. Zeus ran up to him and offered a wet kiss on the cheek in greeting.

Prad smiled, knowing that if Zeus liked this man, he was in good hands. He also thought it best to believe Bernadette about the size of his bump. After all, she could make walls open and magic men step out.

"Hello, Pádraig. My name is Aloysius. I hear you have had a bit of an accident. I am here to make you feel better. Is that agreeable to you?"

Prad gently nodded his consent.

Aloysius looked into Prad's eyes. With the tenderest of touch, he brushed back hair so he could see the bump.

"Pádraig, does your head hurt?"

Again, Prad gently nodded.

"Are you sleepy?"

Another nod.

"When you look at me, can you see me clearly? Do you have any ringing in your ears?"

Prad's head moved to signal a "yes" and a "no" answer.

"You are a lucky young man, Master Knez. I will give Bernadette something to ease your discomfort."

Aloysius produced a bottle of ginkgo biloba and a small amount of turmeric from his bag. He instructed Bernadette to ice the bump – 10 minutes on and 10 minute off – for the rest of the afternoon. He also gave her a small bottle of lavender oil, which he instructed her to dab under Prad's nose if he appeared anxious.

"Remember, Bernadette, lavender oil is poison for pets. Do not let the dogs near Prad if you use it on him. No licking allowed."

Aloysius packed up his bag and turned to leave. "Bernadette, there are some mighty nervous people in the study. You might want to use a wee bit of lavendar on them to sooth their nerves."

With a hearty chuckle, he was gone. The bookcase moved back into place as if Aloysius had been a mere figment of the imagination.

As Bernadette tucked the blankets around Prad, she reminded him of his promise not to mention Aloysius. "People would not understand. He is our secret."

Prad smiled a conspiratorial grin.

"I believe Dr. Adair is here to see you now."

Prad's smile grew a little wider.

Bernadette opened the bedroom door to allow Dr. Adair access. She and the good doctor exchanged pleasantries, and Bernadette explained that she was just about to fetch ice for Prad's head.

"That is a wise decision. Of course, I expect nothing less from you. You always seem to have every situation under control no matter how minor or major it may be."

Bernadette blushed and flattered the good doctor by saying that she had learned much from watching him over the years. Now, it was the doctor's turn to smile. He turned and approached Prad, who stirred from his slumber. Dr. Adair asked him to explain what had happened, which Prad did in great detail.

"I have a suggestion to you, young man. Next time, get a cap with a strap!"

A belly laugh followed as he instructed Prad to lie back. Like Aloysius, he told Prad that he was a lucky lad. He advised him to remain in bed for a few days and to do absolutely everything Bernadette told him to do.

The doctor and Bernadette bid Prad goodbye. Together, they ambled down the stairs to give the adults an update.

Mazie and Hera took this as their cue to go upstairs and visit Prad. The little girl tiptoed out of the library and hurried up the stairs at a fast, but quiet speed. Hera was at her heels. Both the human friend and the canine companion walked up to Prad's bed and stared down at him. Prad, feeling eyes upon him, stirred awake. Seeing Mazie, he offered a wispy hello.

"How are you feeling, Prad?"

"My head hurts and I am very tired. I think my eyesight has been affected. I could swear there were two doctors in the room. Bernadette was with them. One of the doctors was a very small man."

Mazie covered her mouth so as not to be heard laughing by her parents. "Prad, you met one of the Knights. His name is..."

Hearing adults coming up the stairs, Mazie bent forward and whispered in Prad's ear. "Remember Prad, they are a secret."

There was no way to know if Prad heard her or if he remembered the warning. By the time the Boyles and his parents entered the room, he was fast asleep.

CHAPTER SIXTEEN

"Difficult roads often lead to beautiful destinations."
~ Unknown ~

*W*hen Prad awoke the next morning, he was certain of two things. One, his head hurt and, two, someone was in the room with him. Raising his head cautiously off the pillow, he looked across the room and saw Aloysius perusing the books on the shelves.

"Good morning, Pádraig. How are you feeling today?

"My head hurts and I am hungry."

"A joy to my ears, boy... the hunger not the hurt. Drink some water." Aloysius poured a glass and handed it to Prad. "I heard Bernadette puttering in the kitchen so food should be here shortly."

Aloysius told Prad that he had been waiting behind the bookcase for some time... waiting for Prad's parents to leave. He said that he recognized their concern for their son.

"You are a lucky young man in more ways than one. Your parents are good, kind people. They love you deeply."

Before Prad could answer, Bernadette entered the room carrying a tray laden with the most delicious smelling assortment of breakfast foods. She was followed by two four-footed creatures whose nails clicked on the floor as they walked. Zeus and Hera needed to see for themselves that Prad was on the mend.

Prad roused himself and sat up. Aloysius held up a hand for Bernadette to wait while he examined the bump again. Satisfied with what he saw, he said "Eat hearty."

Aloysius said, "Bernadette, those two grand animals gave you away. For I know it is a rare day when you do not have the prowess of a cat."

As Bernadette put the tray in front of Prad, she asked Aloysius for an update on his condition. Learning that the boy was fine and would only need one more day of rest, she gave Aloysius a hug of gratitude.

As Bernadette and Aloysius continued talking, Prad devoured the fruits, scones and cereal in front of him. In between chews, he listened to the banter between the two long-time friends. Only when he heard them mention a visit to the village did his interest pique.

"Village? What village?" he asked with his mouthful.

"Pádraig," Bernadette often addressed Prad by his Gaelic name, "I realize you have many questions about Aloysius. On the morrow, those questions will all be answered."

Prad felt almost instantly better. He had to keep himself from jumping out of bed and was not sure how he would get through the day without bursting.

The four-legged warning system suddenly went into action. Zeus and Hera began to prowl the room and sniff at the door. Aloysius disappeared into the bookcase a second before Owen and Juliana entered.

"Oh, look at himself sitting up in bed being waited hand and foot like a prince," said Owen. To which Juliana added. "And after yesterday, I would have it no other way. How are you feeling today, Prad?"

Prad assured his hosts that he was feeling fine and was looking forward to being out of bed the next day. Bernadette confirmed that Prad was recovering quickly. Owen told Prad that Flynn had been given an extra good rub down as a reward for his service and Zeus had eaten like a king, but being the gentleman that he is, he shared with Hera.

CHAPTER SEVENTEEN

*"Let us always meet each other with a smile, for the smile is the
beginning of love."*
~ Mother Teresa ~

he Irish *Muintir na hÉireann* are an ethnic group native
to the island of Ireland who share a common identity
and culture. They are a nation unto themselves, living on a rock
island that was formed millions of years ago. Since prehistoric
times, humans have roamed this beautiful but sometimes harsh
island. The inhabitants use the raw materials available to them to
build dwellings, make clothing, hunt, farm, make music and bury
their dead.

From Ireland's pagan past to its conversion to Christianity in
or around the 5th century, the Knights have been a constant. They
are a kind and peaceable people, who prefer to remain Ireland's
secret clan. Knights are both male and female. They have been a
not so visible part of the past and present landscape of Ireland.
The Knights are masters of disguise, able to blend in wherever life

takes them. Through the centuries they have knowingly and unknowingly been at the side of the world's greatest minds. While they are of superior intellect, they prefer a peaceful and tranquil life over all else.

Throughout Ireland and the world, there were undisclosed villages where the Knights lived by their own set of rules. Their days were filled with hard work and an earnest desire to do good deeds for others.

The village to which Aloysius belonged was situated on a parcel of land in Glenties, County Donegal, owned by Owen and Juliana Boyle. Their existence was known only to Bernadette and Mazie. Hidden in plain sight under what appeared to be a mammoth bramble patch, access to the village could only be made through the Boyles' stables, a few underground tunnels, some well-hidden paths and passageways inside the house.

Bernadette had been a friend to the Knights since she was a small girl. Her introduction to the Boyle family had not been a matter of coincidence. When it was discovered that the Boyles had purchased the land upon which the Knight's village stood and were planning to build a house, steps were taken to secure their lifestyle.

As it was understood that the Boyles' constant presence could jeopardize the continuance of secrecy, Bernadette was sent to act as protector. She became both governess and head housekeeper for the Boyle family, thereby guaranteeing that the Knights would not be found.

Without the Boyles being aware, the specifications for the house included upgrades which would allow the Knights to come and go undetected. That is how Aloysius was able to visit Prad with only Prad, Mazie and Bernadette knowing of his arrival and departure.

The Boyles' home was an important cog in the wheel for the Knights. County Donegal had long been called the forgotten county, making it the perfect place for the Knights' way of life. No one wanted a revelation of sorts to announce their presence.

Being scholars of the highest degree, the Knights and their

ancestors had been schooled by the greatest minds to ever exist. Not only could they recite the works of William Shakespeare, they could tell you what he ate for breakfast.

The Knights held a tremendous respect for the earth. They studied the ways of the Aztecs, Egyptians and advanced societies throughout the world. When planning their villages, they relied on the principles they had learned from these long-dead civilizations. Whenever possible, they replicated what those brillant minds of the past had created.

While the Knights were a secret to most of the world, they were a caring and loving clan to each other. They encouraged each other in life's endeavors and were fiercely loyal. If they knew of a clan member living in a part of the world where they would be traveling, they sought them out.

The Knights were individualists. They strove for originality in everything. Smiling was as natural to them as breathing. Once a non-Knight person was accepted by them, they became an honorary Knight.

Pradraig Knez was to become the next inductee. From the first time Bernadette met Prad, she knew he had what it took to be a Knight. The harsh fall that caused Prad to hit his head necessitated an earlier than planned introduction. There was no better way to explain Aloysius than with the truth.

Dressed and ready to leave the house, Prad sat on the edge of his bed. His nervous hands had him smoothing and re-smoothing his tweed pants over and over again. He tugged constantly at his white linen shirt. And... his mind raced.

Who was Aloysius? Where did he come from? What was the village? Where was it? And where were Bernadette and Mazie. Mazie? Why was she coming along. Did she already know about Aloysius?

Just as he thought his head would explode with unanswered questions, his bedroom door opened and Zeus and Hera appeared. Bernadette and Mazie were but a step behind.

"So, Pádraig, what are your plans for today?" Prad's face fell and Bernadette and Mazie dissolved into squeals of laughter.

Bernadette explained to the children that they only had so much time. She had given the other adults tasks to do, but they would soon enough have them completed and be looking for the rest of the family.

Bernadette motioned for Mazie to check that the bedroom door was closed. She walked to the bookcase, touched it gently and, like magic, it opened to reveal a long hallway leading down toward the basement. With a beckoning finger, she motioned for Prad to follow her into the secret passage. Once Mazie and the dogs were through, the bookcase closed behind them.

CHAPTER EIGHTEEN

"It is not so much our friends' help that helps us as the confident
knowledge that they will help us."
~ Epicurus ~

*Z*eus and Hera led the way, their confidence registering
that they had made this trip many times in the past.
After what seemed like a never-ending journey, they came to a
door. Bernadette opened it, revealing an elevator. As the elevator
descended, Prad noticed there were none of the sounds usually
associated with a traction lift. The earth around them was eerily
quiet.

"Pádraig, I know you have been hanging on like a loose button.
Your desire to know all there is to know about the Knights is
written across your face. Well, lad, your time has come."

The elevator stopped and Bernadette opened the door. A tiny
Irish village was revealed. The dogs ran out as the villagers ran in
to greet them. Bernadette and Mazie were hugged by everyone in
the crowd.

Mazie gripped Prad's hand and led him a distance away from the gathering. She told him how happy she was to no longer need to keep the secret of the Knights from him. As they walked further into the village, residents came out of their homes and stores to issue a warm welcome. They treated Prad as though they had know him for years... which in some ways, they had. Just as they reached a bend in the road, Aloysius appeared. He shook Prad's hand warmly and inquired about his head. Prad assured him he was fine.

Aloysius was a handsome bespeckled man. The top of his head brushed the underside of Prad's chin. His wavy brown hair was so thick it added another inch to his diminutive stance. Aloysius' entire body was perfectly proportioned, a surprising realization for Prad.

Surveying the village and its inhabitants, Prad was surprised to see that everyone – from the youngest to the oldest – was a perfect specimen of a human being. The only difference was that no one appeared to be taller than four foot.

Bernadette gathered Mazie, Prad and the dogs and set out on a guided tour. She led her little group to the one building that stood high above the rest. It was the library, and people were coming and going, their arms filled with at least one book to read and those that had already been read.

Upon entering, Prad saw a man and a woman standing at the counter. There was a long line of people waiting patiently to see them. Everyone seemed to be acquainted with the couple and they, in turn, greeted everyone by name. Bernadette pointed to the end of the line and motioned for Prad and Mazie to wait there.

Prad was fascinated by the respect that was being shown to these two people. Most of the visitors carried bouquets of flowers. There were already six vases filled to overflowing on the desk.

Waiting on line directly in front of Prad was a little girl. When she reached the counter, she handed the woman flowers, saying "Mrs. Welsh, thank you and Mr. Welsh for helping me locate the books on Germany. I now understand where my Uncle has gone and what he will see while he is there."

Mrs. Welsh's blue eyes sparkled as she replied, "Well, my dear Bridget, I cannot thank you enough for your thoughtfulness in bringing these beautiful flowers. Would you be so kind as to tell us what each of these flowers might be?"

The little girl beamed with pride. She asked, "Do you want to know their botanical name or common English name?"

Mr. And Mrs. Welsh answered together, "Common name, please."

Bridget began her recitation. "This is the oxeye daisy. This is the cuckoo flower. This bright yellow one is a creeping buttercup."

There was polite applause from Mr. And Mrs. Welsh and those book lovers within earshot. Bridget bowed and took her exit, a smile spreading across her face.

Bernadette stepped forward and greeted the couple. "Hello, Catherine. Hello, Bill. It is my pleasure to introduce a fine young man... Pádraig Knez."

Catherine and Bill warmly welcomed Prad with a strong shake of his hand. Then, they gave a cheery "Hello" to Mazie and the dogs. Catherine took a few carrots from her apron pocket, which she fed to Zeus and Hera. "Such good dogs, you are!"

"Pádraig," Bernadette said, "I have it on good authority that Catherine knows the location of every book in every library in County Donegal. Bill, I am told, knows what is inside of each of those books."

The couple blushed at the compliment as Catherine held Prad in her gaze.

"Pádraig, you are not unknown to us. Bernadette speaks very highly of you. We are pleased to welcome you to our family. Mazie, Zeus and Hera joined us some time ago. It is always a pleasure when they come to visit." Catherine patted the dogs on the head and gave each of them another carrot.

"I am amazed by the beauty of your village and the friendliness of the people. I have traveled a bit but never met anyone quite like each of you. I am grateful to have the opportunity to get to know you."

"Thank you for your kind words. We will not keep you any longer. You must start on your journey before it gets late."

Catherine ushered Prad and Mazie toward a collection of books that were voluminous in size and number. She explained that these books were both fiction and non-fiction and that they had been published within the last 10 years. Next to each large book was a smaller book.

"In here," she explained, "are notes made by a Knight who was lucky enough to be with the author as he or she was writing."

Prad's eyes grew immense. "A Knight was with the author while the book was being written?"

"Indeed," Catherine answered, a forced solemnity in her voice. "Come this way, please."

At the end of the room was a large auditorium. Catherine explained that this was the village meeting hall and also served as the theater when shows were produced. With a giggle and a smirk, she told Prad that there was a second location for meetings and shows -- The Red Hand Pub.

"I think you would enjoy visiting there before you leave today.

Everywhere Prad looked there were maps and globes... some covering the tops of tables from end to end. Others were pinned to the walls. Prad was reminded of Owen Boyle's office, which also had maps of the world on the walls and globes on any number of desks. At the tables sat quite a large number of people who appeared to be doing research and writing down their findings in special notebooks.

Bernadette explained that Knights had a thirst for knowledge. The notes Prad saw them taking would one day become part of a discussion. The library had many different rooms where the Knights would meet to discuss various subjects. They did this so they could learn from each other's experiences.

Prad saw Bridget, the little girl with the flowers, staring up at one of the maps. She noticed Prad looking at her.

"That's a map of Europe. My Uncle Cornelius is traveling to Germany. The maps are how we follow his journey. It makes us feel as though we are traveling with him."

Without hesitation, Prad pointed to Croatia on the map. "This is my home. I left there with my parents a few months ago. Soon we will travel to..." Prad looked around at the walls until he found a map of the States. "... soon we will travel here."

Bridget thanked Prad for sharing this part of his life with her. She curtsied and ran off to where her mother was waiting.

CHAPTER NINETEEN

"Life was meant for good friends and great adventures."
~ Unknown ~

*P*rad watched Bridget as she returned to her mother's side. There was a look of wistfulness on his face. He was missing home and the simple life he had lived in Croatia. Catherine recognized the memories that were coursing through Prad's mind... memories that stirred strong feelings, and she set about trying to distract him.

"Pádraig, I would like to tell you a simple truth about the Knights. While we have accomplished great deeds over the centuries, we are also proud of the small efforts we make to show our gratitude for nature's gifts. Come. I want to show you something."

Catherine motioned to Bill, pointing to a box on a nearby desk. In the box were many frames and vases of varying sizes.

Bill held one of the frames up for Prad to see. "The Knights do not believe in waste. All the vases of flowers that we receive are tokens of appreciation, tokens which come from the heart. We take pieces of the different flowers and encase them in a frame.

Sometimes, we turn those flowers into pins, which our people wear proudly on their shirts and give as gifts. The frames and the pins are made by our craftsman using metal and glass from their workshops."

"You may have noticed, Pádraig," Catherine added, "that your mother has been wearing a small pin with a burst of meadow sweets inside. Mazie gave those flowers to me as a thank you for helping her to research Dalmatians, a breed of dog which originated in your homeland. When you and your family arrived, Mazie asked if a few of the flowers could be put into a pin for your mother. She adores your mother. We were happy to make that happen.

By saving small bits and pieces of nature's bounty, we are able to make beautiful memories that will, hopefully, join all peoples – Knights and commoners - to one another."

Bernadette then reminded the children that she had to get them home before their parents realized they were gone. She promised that they would return on the morrow. Feeling as if they had known Catherine and Bill forever, Prad and Mazie wrapped their arms around them in a farewell hug.

Prad babbled non-stop all the way home. He never stopped to take a breath, not even as they rode the elevator up or while they made their way back along the hidden passage. Bernadette and Mazie let him talk right up to the moment that Bernadette prepared to push open the bookcase. With a finger to her lips, she reminded him nicely but sternly that the secret of the Knights needed to be protected.

During dinner that evening, Mazie and Prad listened with interest as Bernadette gave their parents suggestions for how to spend the following day. They realized that she was securing the morning hours for their return to the village.

As the sun came over the horizon, Prad got dressed and then paced his room as he waited anxiously for the day to begin. He had taken special pains with his appearance, wanting to make a good impression on everyone he would meet in the Village. Bernadette and Mazie arrived with Zeus and Hera on their heels.

"You are looking quite spiffy today, young Pádraig." Bernadette's compliment caused the color to heighten on Prad's cheeks. She turned away quickly so as not to embarrass him further.

In less time than it takes to blink, the bookcase opened and off they went on another adventure. Just as they had the day before, the villagers stopped to greet them warmly. Being familiar with the path to the library, Prad was able to slow his step and take notice of the different workshops. He was surprised to see women wearing pants and doing skilled work that would normally be done by men.

When they reached the library, they found the Welshes in their usual place behind the desk. Warm and welcoming "Hellos" were exchanged. Catherine mentioned showing Prad the underground lair which she had promised to do the day before. Bill or Catherine would need to be their guide.

"Unfortunately, Bernadette, Catherine and I must take our children to Step Dancing Class. We try never to miss a lesson."

"Oh, my, I had forgotten about dancing class. Would you mind if we postponed the visit to another time." Catherine's dismay was written on her face.

Prad, of course, agreed. He whispered to Mazie, "Underground floors! This village and these people are so much more than I ever imagined."

Mazie politely asked if they could watch the dance class for a little while. When Mr. and Mrs. Welsh gave their consent, she could barely keep her feet from moving to some imagined music. Together they walked to a nearby room.

When the door opened, the voices of happy children greeted them. "Hello, Mr. & Mrs. Welsh."

Catherine and Bill waved back, using both hands. Suddenly,

three little tykes rushed to the Welshes and wrapped their arms around their legs.

"Hi, Ma. Hi, Da."

Remembering their manners, the children said, "Hello" to Bernadette and Mazie before burying their heads in Zeus' and Hera's fur.

"Pádraig," Catherine said, "I would like for you to meet our children. This is our son, Willie. He is the oldest. This young lady is our daughter, Peggy, and this little fellow is our youngest, Jimmy."

Prad waved, then shook their hands. Willie, who had blond hair and brown eyes, was closest to Prad's and Mazie's age. Peggy was 10 and had brown hair and brown eyes. Jimmy had red hair and brown eyes. He looked to be around seven and seemed a bit shy, but when his father asked how the day was going, he eagerly joined his brother and sister in describing what they had learned about dinosaurs.

Willie told Prad, "We have been studying Croatia so we could know more about your homeland."

Jimmy chimed in, "Your dogs have spots!"

"I know your dogs are called Dalmatians," Peggy added, "but is it true that when they are born, they are all white?"

Prad assured her that what she had read was true.

Willie rejoined the discussion. "We also read that there once were dinosaurs in Croatia. I believe they were called sauropods."

Catherine and Bill gathered their children and the guests together saying, "We can discuss all this later. Now, it is time for dance class. Let us go."

The auditorium was not empty when they arrived. Five other children waited for class to begin. Almost immediately, music filled the air.

Prad looked around for whomever was playing the music, but he saw no one. As they got closer to the stage, the music got louder. Again, Prad looked around and this time saw what appeared to be a box with sound. He was mesmerized and his reaction did not go unnoticed by the Welsh children.

"That's a gramophone," Peggy said and went on to explain that Gerry, the handiest of all the Knights, had made it. "When Gerry was in the United States, he visited Thomas Edison's home and took notes of all the things he was doing. Gerry can rig anything that needs to be rigged."

Willie agreed and Jimmy gave a positive grunt. Prad said he would be pleased to meet this Gerry who can rig so well.

Just then, a man named Danny jumped on stage. "Gather round, kiddies. Class is beginning."

The children scampered into place, tallest (Willie) to shortest (Jimmy).

"Time for me to see who has been practicing as you were instructed to do. Those of you who have put in the time and effort will be rewarded by spending Pirates Day on the boat with Captain Ed." He cranked up the gramophone and the music began to play.

The children stood with their arms stiff against their sides. Their feet began to move, but their upper bodies remained rigid. Even Jimmy, whose feet were so much smaller than those of the other children, performed beautifully.

From their heels to their toes, with knees high in the air, the dancers moved in perfect unison across the stage. When the music stopped, Bernadette, Mazie, and Mr. and Mrs. Welsh applauded enthusiastically. Prad, who was entranced by what he had seen, clapped hardest of all.

Danny sang their praises, a lilt in his voice. He acknowledged that they had all been working hard and assured them that when they competed against other Knight communities, they would be the winners.

"I have no doubt you will all be aboard the Blake Kelsey with Captain Ed and, God willing, he will not make any of you walk the plank." Danny laughed as the children cheered and begged to dance a little more.

Bernadette raised her hand to get the children's attention. She asked if they would like to see another little girl dance, someone not in their troupe.

A voice coming from behind Bernadette was heard to say, "Oh, no. Please, no."

The children turned to look at Mazie. Their eyes pleaded with her to join them on stage. She relented, which brought a huge smile to Prad's lips.

Danny once again wound the gramophone and started the music. Mazie stood as stiff and tall as she could at center stage. She looked at Bernadette for encouragement.

Bernadette flashed a big smile and a nod that said "You can do this."

Mazie had been rehearsing a special themed dance for weeks. The determination on her face attested to the depth of her focus.

She began to move with a precision that was beautiful to watch. Her legs swept through the air and her feet moved with the speed of lightning, telling a story with each tap against the wood floor. By the time the last note sounded, everyone was cheering.

Catherine exclaimed, "Mazie, where did you learn to dance with such grace?"

Mazie pointed to Bernadette, who began to blush.

The inquiring look on Mrs. Welsh's face forced Bernadette to confess. She explained that her mother had been a dance teacher in Longford, the city where she had grown up. With modesty, she revealed that she had won county competitions every year. Now that she was too old to raise her legs and move her feet as quickly as she had once done, it was time for Mazie and the other children to carry on the tradition.

Danny asked if she would dance just a little bit for them and Bernadette promised "Perhaps, another day."

With the clap of her hands, she gathered Mazie, Prad, Hera and Zeus and set about getting everyone home safely.

CHAPTER TWENTY

"Cowards die many times before their deaths; the valiant never taste death but once."
~ William Shakespeare ~

Once back in the bedroom, Prad looked from Bernadette to Mazie and back again. All he could stammer was, "You... You... You..." to which the two ladies responded with a huge laugh.

"You learned a lot today, Master Pádraig. Never forget that you have been entrusted with a great secret," Bernadette reminded her young charge as she left to begin preparations for the evening meal.

"Mazie, you were amazing. I have never seen dancing like that. The other kids were good, but you were great. Your legs... how did you raise them so high and straight?"

Mazie blushed and covered her embarrassment by promising to have Bernadette teach Prad how to dance. "She is a wonderful teacher, Prad. She could teach a scarecrow to do the jig."

Prad scratched his head. He realized that his father's powers of observation were right. The boat *Blake Kelsey* was equipped for people of regular and smaller stature. He now realized the smaller stature people were the Knights, specifically Captain Ed and his passengers. He remembered walking past someone in the village wearing a sea captains hat.

Prad asked if there was a gramophone in the house and when Mazie told him there was one in the library, he asked if he could look at it.

"Have you ever met Gerry, Mazie? He sounds like a fascinating person."

Mazie laughed. "Gerry is the person who built the elevator you rode on to reach the village. All the Knights are intelligent, but Gerry is a super genius. You will meet him soon. I want to be there when you do so I can see the look on your face."

Before Prad could ask what she meant, Mazie opened the bedroom door and motioned for him to follow her downstairs.

As Mazie and Prad approached the library, they could hear the adults talking. Owen was telling Stjephan and Vesna about the Dingle Peninsula and the Blasket Islands in the southwest of Ireland. From the tone of the conversation, it sounded as though a trip was being planned.

Over dinner, the children learned that Owen and Juliana had arranged with a distant relative to use his small house near the Blasket Islands for a mini-vacation. The Earl of Cork, as the relative was known, was the landlord for the islands. Owen and Juliana planned to use the trip to bring gifts for the Presentation Sisters in Cork.

The two families agreed to visit the Dingle Peninsula together. When they returned to Glenties, the Knez family would leave for London so they could bid farewell to Patrick before sailing off to America.

While preparations were being made for the trip, Prad spent the time taking the secret passage to the Village. He no longer needed a chaperone. Whenever he went to the Village, he stopped to talk with the Welshes. He also kept his eyes open for a chance to meet Gerry.

Unfortunately, at Bernadette's insistence, Gerry had gone to Letterkenny to help with the building of the Cathedral. He was gone longer than expected due to the crowds of people who stood watching the construction day after day. Gerry was having a difficult time remaining unseen by prying eyes.

When not in the Village or with his parents, Prad spent time with Mazie. She was not only practicing the piano with him but also teaching him some simple dance steps. When Bernadette was nearby, he plied her with endless questions almost to the point of exhaustion on her part. In desperation, she suggested he go with his mother to meditate at the shrine of the Blessed Mother. The shrine was located on the river, one of the most beautiful spots in the landscape.

Vesna spent time every morning saying the rosary on her knees in front of the statue of Mary. Prad arrived after she had already begun her vigil. He approached quietly, marveling at his mother's beauty when seen in quiet invocation.

He knew he was blessed to have such loving and devoted parents. His mother and father were always interested in what Prad was thinking and saying.

His parents showed an interest in everyone who came into their presence. Prad knew that their willingness to accept people outside their normal circle allowed him to explore the world around him and get to know the many new friends he now held dear.

From his place near the river, Prad could see his father riding Sullivan out in the field. In Croatia, Stjephan never relaxed enough to go horseback riding. He was much too busy working.

The family ate dinner together every night and often took walks in the early evening before the air got too cold. They attended church services every Sunday but that was the extent of their socializing. This trip had allowed his father to relax... to let go of the day to day worries of business.

Prad was learning more about his parents during these months away from home, and he liked what he saw. His father thoroughly enjoyed his friendship with Owen, and Vesna was thrilled by her relationship with Juliana. He had grown very fond of Mazie and hoped the Boyles would visit them in Croatia once they returned from America.

Vesna lifted her head to look at the statue and spotted Prad out of the corner of her eye. She smiled, the sight of her son bringing her true joy. Prad hurried to his mother's side and took her hand in his own.

"Mother, this statue of Rosa Mystica is one of your favorites, is it not?"

She shook her head "Yes."

"I am so happy that a copy of this statue will be waiting when we return from our journey. Whenever I see it, I will be reminded of this wonderful trip to Ireland and the wonderful people we have met and come to love. Thank you. Thank father for giving me this gift."

Prad pulled his mother close and gave her a hug. Vesna began to cry and Stjephan, arriving just at that moment, asked what was wrong.

"Tears of joy, my darling husband," Vesna replied. "We are blessed with a kind and thoughtful son."

Stjephan kissed Vesna on the head while smiling his agreement in Prad's direction.

Both families awoke early the next morning. With full bellies, thanks to the delicious breakfast prepared by Bernadette's skillful hands, they settled comfortably in the Boyle's coach. One last look at the house and a goodbye wave to Zeus and Hera, who wagged their tails from the front porch, and they were off.

Due to the distance they would travel and the number of passengers, both Flynn and Sullivan were on duty. The weather offered a mist of rain and a strong breeze off the Atlantic Ocean.

Inside the coach, there was excited chatter about this new adventure. The only question was why Bernadette had not been on the porch with the dogs to wave them "Safe journey."

An hour into their travels, the group stopped in Tralee to deliver the provisions they had brought for the Presentation Sisters in County Cork. The local people, those who worked for the Donegal Railway Company, offered to help get the supplies to the sisters. They would pass the word up the line so that everything arrived quickly and without damage.

Owen suggested they walk around the town for awhile so the horses could get some rest. An item in the window of a jewelry store caught Vesna's eye. She encouraged the others to continue their walk while she went inside to speak with the storekeeper.

The group continued their leisurely walk and then returned to the coach where they waited patiently for Vesna to join them. When she arrived, she told Juliana and Mazie that she had a present for them... a token of thanks for the wonderful hospitality they had shown.

She handed the ladies a small box which contained a gold charm bracelet. On the bracelet was a boat, a train, a dog, a horse pulling a carriage and a heart. She explained that the boat and train represented the modes of transportation they took to reach Ireland, the dog was for Zeus and Hera, the carriage and horse were self-explanatory and the heart was for how much their friendship meant to her, Stjephan and Prad.

Juliana and Mazie were surprised by the beauty and sentiment of the gift. Stjephan remarked that he and Vesna had discussed how they could show their appreciation for the kindnesses shown to them. He was overjoyed that Vesna had found an appropriate gift.

With a neigh from Sullivan and a whinny from Flynn, the happy travelers continued on their way.

CHAPTER TWENTY-ONE

"Without friends, no one would want to live, even if he had all other goods."
~ Aristotle ~

$\mathcal{L}$ate in the day, the carriage arrived at a charming house in Ventry, a small town near the water. Entering the house, Prad and Mazie immediately began roaming from room to room while the horseman brought in two baskets of food prepared by Bernadette. The tired travelers could not decide which made them happier... the comfort of the house or the aroma of delicious food. They decided they were equally grateful for both.

In the morning, the sound of water breaking against the shore and the mew call of seagulls gliding just above the water's surface awoke most everyone. Gathering in the kitchen for breakfast, the group decided the day was perfect for exploring. The beach was first on their list.

Juliana told Vesna she had been informed that a statute of the

Rosa Mystica was enshrined on a nearby cliff. Vesna's excitement grew and she begged Stjephan to take her to see it.

"We can use the rowboat we saw on the beach. Please, Stjephan," she cajoled.

Mazie laughed at the look on Vesna's face and Prad added to his mother's urging by saying he wanted to run on the beach and feel the salt air on his face. The Boyles decided to stay at the house and attend to some chores.

As there was an early morning chill in the air, Prad wore his tweed blazer... the one with the extra pockets sewn into the lining by Bernadette. Vesna asked Prad to keep her ring and pearl bracelet in one of the pockets so she did not lose them. Prad took off his cap and put it in a pocket for safekeeping as well.

Vesna rushed about getting her coat and scarf for the trip. When she rejoined her son and husband who were waiting outside the house, she announced she was "... ready to go."

Stjephan bowed and said, "Your vessel awaits, my lady."

At the beach, Vesna and Stjephan set out in the boat while Prad ran along the shore, stopping from time to time to collect treasures he found in the sand. He would call out to his parents each time he found a razor shell, blue mussel, spotted cowrie, or Kelly green sea glass.

Stjephan and Vesna laughed at seeing their son's joy and, as the waves tossed the boat about, their laughter became louder and more jubilant. Suddenly, a strong squall rolled in, causing the laughter to be replaced by the hushed sounds of wariness. Thunder rumbled overhead. Lightning reached down from the clouds and touched the ground.

As the storm intensified, the world around them went quiet. No birds fly overhead. The seagulls did not squawk. Except for the storm, there were no sounds to be heard. The Knez family had gone silent as well.

Prad looked out to sea, searching for his mother and father. He saw their boat moving toward the statue of Rosa Mystica in the distance, and he jumped up and down, waving his arms to get their attention. Just as he was about to shout their names, the head of a grotesque snake-like creature, many times bigger than any animal Prad had ever seen, rose above the water beside the little boat.

The sea serpent or sea dragon as they are sometimes called was, at least, 20 feet long and 10 feet wide. It was a vile looking creature, with long dagger-like fangs and a bifurcated tongue that appeared to be as long as its body. Adding to the serpent's terrifying appearance were massive fins protruding from the top and sides of its body and from behind its massive head.

Prad screamed a warning, but the roar of the storm drowned out his young voice. As he watched in horror, the serpent's mouth opened and its tongue gripped Vesna and Stjephan, pulling them toward their fate. As the serpent's fangs ripped into his parents, Prad could hear their blood curdling screams and their pleas for mercy.

The rain poured out of the heavens like a sheet of iron. The lightning and thunder filled the air with the sounds of death. The last image Prad saw was his parents in the jowls of the thrashing beast. Then, it dove under the water and the sea grew calm.

Prad ran along the beach until he reached the pathway leading to the statue of Rosa Mystica. He was about to kneel and pray when the creature's tail snaked out of the water and whipped the statue, sending it sailing high into the sky before it crashed into the water below. The power in the tail was such that the current picked Prad up and catapulted him into the water much as if he was a feather on the wind. Prad's lungs deflated as the air was forced from his body. He found himself floating face up in deep water, completely disorientated.

Just as he was about to sink below the surface, a pair of arms lifted him upwards. A boy about his own age, with red hair and green eyes, carried him to safety. Prad gave silent thanks to God and passed out.

Glenn had watched from a distance as the sea serpent attacked Prad's parents. He knew he could not save them, but he could save their son. A strong swimmer, he reached Prad's side and carried him in his arms to a nearby cave. Once safely inside, he removed Prad's blazer, turned him on his side and began pumping the water from his lungs.

Prad began to sputter. Water continued to pump from his chest under Glenn's strong hands. Once, Prad was breathing without distress, Glenn took his leave. Humans were rarely exposed to Merfolk. A Merboy might be too much of a shock for Prad's weakened system. Before Prad opened his eyes and caught sight of him, Glenn wished him well and dove back under the water.

Through the walls of the cave, Prad heard people calling his name. He recognized Owen Boyle's voice. Then, he heard Mazie's frantic scream. Crying and waving, Prad made his way out of the cave. When he reached Owen's side, all he could do was shake his head "No" when asked if his parents had survived.

Prad awoke the next morning confused and disoriented. Try as he might to not think about the events of the day before, in his mind's eye he relived the horror over and over again. He threw off the bed covers, got dressed and ran down to the kitchen where Owen and Juliana were sitting at the table, looking somber.

The dark circles under their eyes added to their haggard appearance and testified to their not having slept. Juliana fixed Prad a light breakfast as Owen told him that a search party had been formed. They had walked the beach and rowed across the water all night but his parents had not been found. The only evidence that they had even set out to sea was wood from the broken boat.

Prad was agitated, wanting to know why they had not allowed him to help in the search. Owen explained that a doctor had arrived and tended to Prad's injuries. He gave Prad a medication which allowed him to sleep.

Juliana sat next to Prad and took his hand in her own. She assured him that all that could be done had been done. In a few hours, they would return to Glenties.

Prad yelled, "No. I have to stay here and continue looking."

Owen knelt beside the chair. "They are gone, Prad. No amount of searching will bring them back."

Prad began to cry. He heard his parents' screams again and his tears flowed harder. Finally, with his anger spent, he collapsed into Juliana's arms and allowed the pain to wash over him.

CHAPTER TWENTY-TWO

"Although the world is full of suffering, it is also full of the
overcoming of it."
~ Helen Keller ~

$\mathcal{T}$he ride back to Glenties was long. While each person carried an unspeakable heaviness in their heart, the sluggish trot of Flynn and Sullivan spoke to their instinctive awareness that something terrible had happened.

As the carriage pulled up to the Boyles' home, Owen and Juliana asked the children to wait outside for a moment while they spoke with Bernadette. Mazie sat beside Prad and held his hand.

Bernadette appeared at the carriage door. She opened it and with one swift movement climbed inside.

"Pádraig, come to me," she said in a gentle whisper.

Prad immediately buried his head in her chest, and Bernadette's shirt became soaked by the weight of his tears.

"My dear child, I have no words. You must know that your parents' love was deeper and stronger than the pain you are feeling. They will always be with you in spirit. That kind of love never dies."

Bernadette pulled Prad closer, wrapping her arms tightly around him.

"You are not alone, Prad. You are loved by many people, especially by those of us with you today. Now, come, let us go inside."

Owen Boyle was in the library, pouring himself a larger than normal drink. At the sound of the front door opening, he looked up and saw Prad, Bernadette and Mazie enter the foyer. With the weight of the world on his shoulders, he walked to Prad's side and embraced him. Through tears that refused to stop flowing, he promised Prad that he and Juliana would take care of him and would attend to all that needed to be done.

Juliana watched the interaction between her husband and Prad from the library doorway. She had been staring at the bracelet Visna had given her the day before... a gift that now held an even greater significance for it came from a dear friend who was no more. She joined Owen at Prad's side and together they reassured him of their love and devotion.

Mazie suggested they all go into the library. Bernadette went to the kitchen to prepare a light meal which would help to soften the ache in everyone's heart by distracting them for a short while. Owen left to tend to the horses while the others gathered together in quiet remembrance of the loved ones lost that day.

When the repast had been eaten, Bernadette ushered Mazie and Prad toward the stairs.

"You must rest. The body, mind and soul needs sleep to heal and grow strong in the face of tragedy. Today has been long and tomorrow will be longer. Prad, keep Zeus and Hera with you for the night. You will not feel so lonely with them by your bed."

Prad stood up and looked at the people gathered around him. "I love you all so much."

Bernadette followed behind Prad and Mazie as they climbed the stairs. Mazie went to her room, and Bernadette followed Prad to his. Just as she was turning down the bed covers, the bookcase opened and Aloysius appeared. He carried a little bag which he put down while waiting for Prad to settle between the sheets.

"I did not know your parents personally, Prad, but I knew them well enough to know they were good natured souls who loved their son. I am saddened for your loss which is a loss for humanity as well."

Prad forced a smile of gratitude for he knew that Aloysius' words were sincere.

"I have some lavender oil which will help you to sleep. Do not allow Zeus or Hera to lick you once it is applied. For them, it is poisonous."

A second later, the little man was gone, leaving nothing but a wisp of a breeze in his wake.

Bernadette applied the lavender oil to Prad's neck and soon he started to get sleepy. He had never known that his mind, body and soul could be so tired all at the same time.

In the early hours of the next morning Prad felt a tap on his shoulder. Bernadette whispered that it was time to get up. She instructed him to hurry and put on comfortable clothes. Not wanting to embarrass the boy, she left but returned within 10 minutes. Together, she and Prad stepped into the opening behind the bookcase and descended to the elevator and the stable. Flynn and Sullivan were saddled and waiting.

They mounted and rode out side by side. Prad realized he had never seen Bernadette astride a horse. Having seen the grace with which she had taught Mazie to dance, he was not surprised by her finesse while riding.

As they rode across the open field, Prad saw something large and white in the distance. It appeared to be an oddly shaped ball but, as they got closer, he realized it was a hot air balloon. The look he cast toward Bernadette was filled with questions.

As Bernadette and Prad dismounted, a diminutive man with red hair and a mustache approached them. His clothing was different from that of the other residents of the village. He was wearing a khaki jacket belted at the waist, spurs on his boots and a slouch hat pinned up on the side.

Prad recognized that the style of the hat resembled the one worn by Theodore Roosevelt. In fact, everything about this man – his posture, his bearing, his coloring – everything except his size was in perfect imitation of the famous statesman and conservationist. Prad made a mental note that he was in the company of a cowboy Knight.

Holding himself ramrod straight, the man stuck out his hand and introduced himself. "Hello, Pádraig, I am Gerry. Would you like to see the sun rise from my balloon? I call her the Shamrock Express."

Prad returned the handshake while stuttering his affirmative response. Without turning to look at Bernadette, he handed her the reins to his horse and followed Gerry to where the balloon was anchored. Together, they climbed aboard the wicker basket that would carry them up to the clouds.

CHAPTER TWENTY-THREE

"Growth is the only evidence of life."
~ John Henry Newman ~

*G*erry adjusted valves and pushed buttons. Prad felt the basket lift off the ground. Soon, they were flying above the earth. Prad could see Bernadette standing next to Flynn and Sullivan, waving at them. Turning to his left, he saw the Boyles' house nestled between the trees.

When they reached a certain altitude, Gerry explained that they would head north away from the wind for a quarter of an hour. Then, they would turn back and land in the exact spot from which they had departed.

Gerry was an excellent guide, pointing out the villages and towns, some of which Prad had never visited or heard mentioned. He pointed out the spire of the cathedral and, for a brief moment, Prad's heart hurt. This was the cathedral his mother had often spoken about.

As the sun rose higher, its rays caressed the cathedral's stained glass windows, sending a rainbow of brilliant colors up to greet them. Off to the east, a city was coming to life, its citizens looking like ants bustling below. That city was Belfast. Seeing Ireland from this height was almost mind boggling.

As Prad listened to Gerry speak, he felt a thrill like never before. Even so, it was the warm air rushing past his cheeks that made him feel most alive. He silently thanked his parents for the opportunities they had given him.

Gerry turned some levers and pulled on the ropes, turning the balloon back toward home.

"I must get you back, boy, or Bernadette will make me fanny as red as my hair."

Prad giggled and, for a moment, the happiness in his voice caused him pain. Then, he saw the sheep and the cows in the fields and realized that his life must go on. It was what his parents would want for him.

As they descended into the field, Prad looked at his pilot with complete and utter gratitude. He could not believe what he had just experienced... not the man or the ride.

As Prad and Gerry stepped out of the basket, Gerry said, "I was very sorry to hear of your parents passing. There are matters of life you must attend to, but when you return to Glenties, you and I will have a great deal of work to do."

Again, he shook Prad's hand as those closing a business deal.

Bernadette and Prad remounted their horses. As they rode away, Prad looked back to make sure that the past few hours had not been a dream. He knew he could not speak of the balloon ride to anyone. This was another secret that must be kept. He would protect it with his life, if necessary.

Riding up a path near the house, Prad guided his horse to the grotto. Bernadette followed him. He dismounted and walked to where the Rosa Mystica seemed to be holding out her arms to him in welcome. He sensed Bernadette watching him with concern.

"We were all here together the other day," he said, his voice barely above a whisper.

"Yes, my young friend, you were. This grotto will always be the place where you come to count your blessings. Here, you can give thanks for those who love you and those you love. This grotto is your root. It will keep you safely planted with us in Ireland."

Prad understood. He felt those figurative roots growing into the soil. He began to feel stronger. He had new resolve. It was time to take care of those matters which Gerry had mentioned. His steps, as he walked his horse to the stable, were filled with determination.

The next few days were a blur. There was much to do before traveling to England. First, there would be a trip to Letterkenny and a visit with Bishop O'Donnell at the cathedral. The Bishop had sent his condolences and asked that Prad come to see him. The Boyles felt Vesna and Stjephan would approve so the family agreed. At the cathedral they attended a private mass, filled with words of comfort from the Bishop.

From Letterkenny, they traveled to Belfast and boarded the Cunard's private boat. London was their destination. There, they gave Uncle Patrick the tragic news. Prad saw the devastation in his uncle's face.

The hardest part of the trip was still ahead. Arriving in Primosten, he struggled with telling his maternal grandparents of his parents' demise.

Finally, they arrived in Solin.

~

Arriving home after an emotionally and physically debilitating trip, Prad let the Boyles into his house. No soon had he stepped through the doorway than Jupiter and Juno came running.

The Boyles and the dogs treated each other as old friends. Tatiana arrived and, after hugging Prad in welcome, she asked why he was home so soon. When she saw the Boyles, she knew something was wrong.

Prad made the proper introductions. Owen Boyle told Tatiana

that Prad had spoken of her many times. Then, with great empathy, he explained why they were all there.

Tatiana turned to Prad and their eyes met across the room. She ran to him and wrapped her arms around his neck. No words were needed.

Uncle Patrick appeared in the doorway. He had traveled with the Boyles from London. Tatiana used his arrival as an opportunity to run home and get her parents. No one had noticed the elderly man who now stood in the center of the room. Prad's grandfather looked lost. He knew something devastating had happened.

Uncle Patrick kissed his father on both cheeks and suggested that they go into the library to talk. Less than five minutes passed. Prad's grandfather returned, looking older than when he left the room.

He put his hands on his grandson's shoulders and assured him that "This old captain will see you through."

He went away, sadness in his steps, to tell the news to his wife.

Over the next few days, neighbors and friends came to pay their respects. For the memorial service at the family church, two coffins stood side by side in the center aisle. Prad had chosen items from the house that he felt his mother and father would want with them in the afterlife. He included two portraits... one of Vesna and one of Owen. The coffins were placed in the family crypt.

Back home after the service, Prad felt himself called to the garden. Once there, he saw that the statue of the Rosa Mystica which he had brought from Ireland had been placed where the sun shone brightest. A bench had been set in front of it. Shamrocks and Donegal wildflowers had been planted at its base.

Prad sat on the bench and began to speak to his mother and father. No one was near enough to hear him. He cried as he told them of the depth of his love and how lost he felt without them. Then, he wiped his tears and returned to the house where a large crowd waited to see him. Tables had been set up and the food was plentiful.

Not knowing how the food and guests had come together, Prad headed to the kitchen where he found Bernadette, Catherine, Bill and Aloysius dressed in catering clothes.

"Pádraig, do not just stand there," Bernadette ordered. "There are dishes to be set on the tables and glasses to be filled."

Prad was never so happy to be given an order in his whole life. He readily obeyed.

Owen and Juliana watched Prad as he hurried from kitchen to dining room with platters of food. When he paused to take a breath, they explained that Bernadette had insisted on handling the memorial meal while still in Glenties. She had made all the arrangements, including hiring the kitchen help. How she did it they did not know, but they never doubted that she would do what she said she would do.

When all the guests had gone home, Mazie took Prad by the arm and led him into the library where his grandparents, the Boyles and Bernadette waited. He was barely into the room when he was forced to stop short.

On an easel was a framed painting of Prad standing behind his parents. Jupiter and Juno sat at their feet. Bernadette explained that the painting was a gift from friends in Glenties.

When Prad looked at her questioningly, she said, "You may not remember meeting my friends, Prad, but they remember you. When they heard what happened to your mom and dad, they wanted to do something special for you."

Prad was amazed by the detail in the painting. The portraits were exact likenesses of him, his parents and the dogs. His grandfather and Uncle Patrick agreed.

"Exact likenesses, for sure. Miss Bernadette has very talented friends. Generous, too."

Uncle Patrick asked Prad if they could speak privately about his future.

"My future is in this room, Uncle Patrick. I have decided to return to Ireland with the Boyles. At the start of the next school term, I hope you will help to find me a school in London where I can be close to you. When there is no school, I will divide my time between Solin and Glenties."

The adults expressed their admiration for the decisions which Prad had made. They agreed that his choices were the best for him at this time. Uncle Patrick and Owen Boyle would handle all legal matters and Captain Knez would oversee Stjephan's business.

Uncle Patrick also informed Prad that he had a rather large inheritance, all from his father's business and personal assets. Prad, at his young age, was now worth more than many men combined who had worked their whole lives.

CHAPTER TWENTY-FOUR

"Keep your eyes on the stars and your feet on the ground."
~ Theodore Roosevelt ~

*B*ack in Glenties, Prad went to work for Gerry. There was much to learn.

First, Gerry taught him how to care for a hot air balloon. Making sure that everything was in tip top shape before launching was a necessity if accidents were to be avoided. Prad was surprised to learn that there were different types of balloons and each balloon required a different type of fabric.The fabric had to constantly be checked for loose stitching and tears.

Prad learned how to thread a needle, make a perfect stitch and tie a proper knot. He studied both aerostatics and aerodynamics and learned about the different gases that could be used to lift the balloons.

The one job which Prad did not like was cutting through the sharp bramble bushes to find the strong canes needed to make the baskets. He quickly learned how to avoid being stuck by thorns.

Next in his apprenticeship was learning the fine art of weaving and sanding. Any excess branches were made into wreathes and given as gifts for the homes of Knights near and far.

Blacksmithing and welding became two of Prad's favorite jobs. He learned how to choose the proper grade of metal to make the frames for the balloons, and he also learned how to shoe horses. Prad always made sure Flynn and Sullivan got more than enough attention.

The Boyles often inquired what Prad did with his free time. He explained that he enjoyed exploring the surrounding countryside. Sometimes, he said, he would go into town and talk with the shop owners. On one of these trips, he bought a beautiful bramble wreath for Juliana to hang on the front door. Prad could also be found in the stable and Owen was impressed by his interest in and knowledge of horses.

During dinner, Prad, Mazie, Owen and Juliana discussed everything under and above the stars... from Socrates to the outer limits of the universe. The Boyles grew more and more impressed with Prad's ability to talk about matters that should have been far beyond his youthful capabilities. Mazie found the situation and Prad's ability to manipulate her parents amusing.

One day, while checking Sullivan's shoes, Gerry spoke of Colonel Roosevelt. Prad was fascinated and politely asked him about their relationship.

Gerry laughed. "So, you want to know about me and the Colonel, do you?" Prad nodded.

"When I was getting my early education, I read all of the great pieces of literature that Theodore Roosevelt had written. He was a man of superior intellect. I became a great admirer and hoped one day to meet him.

A few years ago, I was sent to America to study the work of Thomas Edison and other great inventors of the day. I have an affinity for electronics and the Knight hierarchy wanted to give me an opportunity to learn from the best.

The wonders that Edison and his associates were developing

were about to change the world. Little did I know that while on a stopover in Montauk, New York, my life would change in a most astonishing way.

I love the world of science, but I am also fascinated by history. A Knight from New York suggested I spend time on Long Island, where many of the early English settlers had lived. The Shinecock Indians, a noble tribe, also lived on Long Island.

An interesting tidbit... at the end of the island is a lighthouse commissioned by George Washington. Imagine. George Washington!

Montauk is a lovely area; not heavily populated so I was able to explore much of the local beauty without interference. One day, there was a great commotion. A tent village popped up without fanfare. Many soldiers on horseback arrived.

I have a bit of a nosy streak so I hung around and listened as the soldiers talked of their escapades. They had just returned from war in Cuba and needed to be quarantined to prevent the spread of malaria and other diseases. Since I had gotten close to them, I had to quarantine as well, which meant hiding in the woods near the tent city.

I was wandering between the tents one night when I heard voices coming close. I took cover, but I was not quick enough and a large man saw me. He told me to "Halt," which I did.

The man did not touch me or threaten me. He stared for a brief moment and we both felt awkward not knowing what to say. I looked for a way to get a conversation going and noticed that the man's glasses were broken.

"I can fix those for you," I said.

The man smiled, and I knew I could trust him. He handed me his glasses which I quickly repaired. My workmanship, as you know, is excellent. The man looked at his glasses and said, "Bully." We became friends at that moment.

That man was Colonel Roosevelt. We sat up most of the night talking and drinking. What conversations we had! We talked of animals, vegetables, minerals and anything else that crossed our minds. I returned each night – in secret, of course – for the next week.

By the time the tent camp moved on, we were close friends. The Colonel gave me his extra slouch hat, the one I am wearing now and rarely take off."

Prad listened to Gerry's story with his mouth half open. When Gerry got to the end, Prad asked how he spent his time after Colonel Roosevelt had left the area. Gerry explained that his interest in the Colonel had grown and he devoted a great deal of time learning all that he could about this amazing man.

"The Colonel had spent a lot of time in the Dakotas, which is where he adopted the safari type of clothing he wore. I decided that I would dress as he dressed in the hope that I could emulate his noble character.

Master Prad, if I may be so bold as to suggest you read every book you can find on the Colonel... those about him and those he wrote himself. Colonel Roosevelt is going to do great things for America. You would be wise to educate yourself for when that time arrives.

Now, back to work or we will get no dinner."

The weeks and months passed quickly with Prad becoming an expert in every trade in the Village. Soon, the days grew shorter, the weather grew cooler and both Gerry and Prad knew it was time for him to leave for London. Another type of schooling awaited his arrival.

The Boyles were sad to see Prad leave, but they were confident his departure was for the best. While Prad did not want to imagine his world without the Boyles, Bernadette or the Knights, he knew he must get on with the matters of life.

Uncle Patrick awaited his nephew's arrival with excitement. He had always longed for a closer relationship with his brother's son. Death was not how he planned for it to happen but he was not one to question fate.

Patrick's house was large. Prad had his own room and a study with large windows that looked out upon a beautiful park.

His uncle had arranged an interview for him with the Head Master of Eton College, which was considered to be the best school in all of England.

Patrick was a powerful man with many important business connections. He had promised that Prad would have the best, and the best was what he would get. After making a few phone calls, Prad received the distinguished label of Oppidan Scholar.

At Eton, there were two distinct categories of students: Collegers were exceptionally smart but had little money and no title. Oppidans had family money and came from upper middle class backgrounds. They were rarely as smart as the Collegers.

There was also a hybrid group known as the Oppidan Scholars. These students were blessed with both brains and money. Prad fell into this category thanks to his Uncle Patrick.

Oppidans were supposed to live in a residence under the watchful eye of an elderly woman or a teacher associated with Eton. Patrick was able to get an exception for Prad, who remained at home in London.

CHAPTER TWENTY-FIVE

"Where we love is home... home that our feet may leave but not our hearts."
~ Oliver Wendell Holmes, Sr. ~

*L*ondon had changed since Prad visited with his parents. It was noisier and dirtier than he remembered. When he and Uncle Patrick visited the zoo, he found that it, too, was different. The exhibits were still fascinating, but with his increased awareness of the ways of the animals, he found certain aspects of their treatment upsetting. He so wished he could talk to the Knights about his observations and get their input.

Dinner was rarely eaten at home. Uncle Patrick frequented London's most premier restaurants. Often, these evenings out were opportunities to introduce Prad to London's elite.

Prad hated being shown about like a prized possession. He knew his uncle meant well, but he saw the look of pity on people's faces and heard the whispering as they talked about his parents' demise. Nothing like that ever happened in Glenties.

Dinner conversations with strangers were often boring business discussions and Prad found himself studying the linen napkins and tablecloths. He would feel for the weight of the fabric and check the stitching. Only when a fellow dinner guest wanted to discuss the great works of literature or art would Prad join the conversation.

The first day at Eton was welcoming and scary. Some of the boys were new, like Prad, but a great many of them were returning students and so knew each other well. Prad followed whatever instructions he was given to make his assimilation go as smoothly as possible. Adhering to the Knights" creed of conduct – *Hide in plain sight* – he went through the day with little difficulty.

In each of his classes, students were given tests to ascertain what knowledge they had retained from the previous term. At the end of the day, Prad and Uncle Patrick were summoned to the Head Master's office.

It came as no surprise that Prad's scores were comparable to those students in their final year at Eton. As the school could not have a young man, especially a newcomer to Eton, test higher than the children of royalty, the best course of action was for Prad to quietly attend advanced classes. At the end of the school year, he would be given final exams and if his grades remained as good as anticipated, he would attend university.

Prad knew that something more than academics was needed for him to succeed in school. Unfortunately, Eton did not have a course in hot air ballooning so his focus had to be shifted closer to the ground.

Uncle Patrick tried to interest him in golf, but the few times he had been on a course had left him bored and disinterested. He did enjoy participating in sporting events and favored three of the newer Olympic competitions. Rowing piqued his interest as it was something he could pursue in solitude.

Prad was pleased to learn that rowing was a serious sport in England. Since he preferred solo activities, he chose to learn single sculling. In single sculling, one rower uses a pair of sculls (oars) to steer the boat by controlling the pressure put on the blades (the flat end of the oar) in the water.

If Prad wanted a social life, he could join the sculling team which was made up of seven rowers and a coxswain. There was also sweep rowing in which one oar was held in two hands. Sweep rowing allowed for as many as eight rowers and a coxswain.

Prad bought a boat and made quiet inquiries to find someone willing to teach him the basics of the sport. He got up early each morning and met his teacher on the banks of the Thames. After only a few lessons, the muscles in his body adjusted to this new sport.

In his first days of practice, Prad felt like a fish out of water. He watched somewhat enviously as experienced rowers glided along the water's surface as if they were one with the river. Prad plodded along.

He studied how the team members held themselves while rowing and began to mimic their posture and movements. Soon, he, too, became one with the water.

Prad looked forward to his mornings on the Thames. From the river, he was able to see the city come to life. He felt himself growing stronger in mind and body. It soon became obvious that, while he was watching the other rowers, they were watching him and liking what they saw.

Friendships developed. He was often asked to join the team, but Prad explained that, for him, rowing was a pleasure, not a competition. He did, however, consent to participating in private matches, which he always won.

Prad wrote often to Bernadette, Gerry, Aloysius and the Welshes. He extolled the benefits of his new hobby. When the Boyles came to visit, which they did about once a month, they saw for themselves how beneficial rowing was for Prad's self-esteem and well being.

Prad cherished his time with Owen and Juliana and knew that they came to London more often than usual because they missed him as much as he missed them. He wished it was possible for Mazie to go along on these trips, but school kept her busy at home.

He wrote to Tatiana every week. He was so appreciative of her care and concern for Jupiter and Juno. Prad missed her and told her in every letter how he looked forward to seeing her when he returned to Solin.

The next time Prad went home to Glenties, there was a surprise waiting for him... a gift from the Knights. The woodworkers had crafted a shell (boat) for his personal use. Of all the shells Prad had seen floating on the Thames, none compared to this gift. He knew the amount of research that had gone into finding the wood and building it to perfection. Prad personally thanked each man and woman who contributed to the finished project.

The boat was christened Knight on Water. Owen and Juliana did not understand the name, but since it made Prad happy, they were pleased. Under the cover of the early morning fog, Gerry, Aloysius, Catherine, Bill and their children cheered Prad on as he practiced. When Owen was able to watch a practice session, he brought Flynn and Sullivan with him.

When Prad went home to Solin, his grandparents had a scull waiting for him. The boat had been made by the workers at Stjephan's company. They christened it Knez III as Prad was a third generation Knez to own a boat.

Prad's grandfather, being the old sea salt that he was, teased Prad that the boat was a bit smaller than what he had expected his grandson to captain. Prad hugged him, knowing that no other response was necessary.

Like his family and friends in Glenties, Tatiana watched the early morning practices. Jupiter and Juno kept her company on the river bank. She would time Prad with a stopwatch and cheer him loudly when he beat his own record.

Whether in Solin or Glenties, Prad spent a little time each day at the feet of the Rosa Mystica, giving thanks for his many blessings.

CHAPTER TWENTY-SIX

"You have brains in your head and feet in your shoes, you can steer
yourself in any direction you choose."
~ Dr. Seuss ~

*T*ime moved with the speed of light. Prad became an
Oxonian, like his Uncle Patrick. He worked hard,
researching different areas of study in an effort to determine his
career path. Early one morning while engaged in his daily rowing
routine, fate led the way.

Prad was about to put his boat into the river when he noticed
the waterfront was eerily still. The usual group of rowers and
trainers were present, but they were standing silently around a
teammate who sat off to the side, bent at the waist and obviously in
pain. His friends were gathered around him, gesturing frantically.

Prad approached and asked what was wrong. The rower told
him that he had excruciating pain in his right side and was feeling
nauseated. Having spent so much time with Aloysius, Prad was
able to make a 99% accurate diagnosis. He asked for permission to

touch the young man's side, which was readily given. The painful response was enough for Prad to ask for someone to bring a bag of ice... "Now!"

While waiting for the ice, Prad explained that the young man needed to get to a hospital. He said he feared the rower's appendix was about to burst. His teammates rushed to secure a ride and then formed a human conveyor belt to get him to the road. One the cab arrived, one teammate climbed in with him while the others followed in their own means of transportation.

Prad's fan club watched from their hiding place in the boathouse. They were in awe of how quickly and calmly he had diagnosed the rower and gotten him help. When Prad arrived at the river to practice the following morning, he was informed by the rower's team captain that his diagnosis had been correct.

The emergency room doctor had told them that the application of ice had kept the appendix from bursting. He said, "You were lucky to have someone with medical knowhow nearby."

Prad was pleased with the acknowledgment. The many hours he had spent with Gerry would always be special to him, but it was the training that he had received from Aloysius that had filled him with a certain sense of pride. Knowing he had helped someone in need was a feeling like none he had ever experienced.

Prad was never unnerved when faced with a medical challenge, whether the injured party was human or animal. He loved healing. He loved seeing a patient go from despair to delighted as they grew healthier. Medicine was his future. Of that, he had no doubt.

The very next time he and Uncle Patrick had dinner together, Prad informed him of his plans. Patrick smiled with pride and encouragement. He assured Prad that his mother and father would be overcome with joy by his decision. Prad thanked him for his vote of confidence.

When the Boyles came for their next visit, Prad waited anxiously to tell them the news. By then, he had already filled out the medical school application and was waiting for his admission interview.

Owen looked from Prad to Juliana, a look of pride so intense on his face that all he could say was, "Our son, the doctor."

"Have you told Mazie or Bernadette, Prad?" Juliana asked.

Prad admitted that he had not thought to do that. He promised he would write each of them *soon.*

"But, in the meantime, if you would tell them when you get home, I would be most appreciative."

When Prad next returned to Glenties, Bernadette had a hero's welcome waiting for him complete with all of his favorite foods. Mazie had made a *Dr. Pádraig Knez M.D.* sign, which she hung on his bedroom door. As wonderful as the celebration offered at the Boyle household, it could not compare to what waited for him at the Knight's village.

Prad could not have been treated with higher respect if he had been responsible for St. Patrick using the shamrock to teach the holy trinity.

Walking into the Village library, he heard Catherine say to Bill, "Husband, a young man has arrived who knows as much as you about all the books in Donegal."

Prad laughed and rushed into their arms for a welcome home hug. Catherine planted a big kiss on his cheek and whispered into his ear how very proud they were of his accomplishment. All Prad could do was blush.

On his way back through the Village, Prad met Aloysius. The healer shook his young charge's hand with great enthusiasm.

"I hear you are planning to outdo me. Soon, there will be an M.D. after your name?"

The old Knight paused and looked at Prad in a somewhat threatening manner.

"Are you planning to be my competition with the villagers?" Aloysius stared at Prad for a minute and then winked to show he was teasing.

Prad laughed with relief. "Oh, no, sir. I could never come close to being the healer you are."

Aloysius knew Prad was sincere. He brushed a tear from his eyes before he could be thought to be a sentimental old fool.

"Pádraig, everyone in the village is proud of you. You have more than fulfilled every expectation we had for your success. We have always been on the outskirts of history, keeping our distance for fear of discovery. You are the first outsider to get close to us. Watching you overcome personal tragedy has taught us so much."

Next for Prad was a stop at Gerry's workshop. Before he even entered the building, Prad could hear Gerry muttering and whistling to himself. He could hear the tinker of tools as Gerry went about whatever project was keeping him occupied.

The sight of Gerry's flaming red hair sticking out from beneath his hat was a warm and welcoming sight. Prad cleared his throat and Gerry looked up.

"I do not remember calling for a doctor!"

Prad laughed and said, "The day you call for a doctor... God help the doctor."

Gerry's face took on a solemn appearance.

"A doctor, eh. That is some profession to pick. Takes courage. Your knowledge and decisions affect others in tremendous ways. But you have had courage from the day we met. You deciding to get in the Shamrock Express and see the sunrise. You were a scrappy thing."

Prad blushed. "I was a scared boy who was lucky enough to have met a cowboy who would show me things I never knew existed. You gave me the courage to take care of those matters in life."

"Well, you're not done yet."

"No, we are not done yet."

CHAPTER TWENTY-SEVEN

Let us be grateful to the people who make us happy; they are the charming gardeners who make our souls blossom.
~ Marcel Proust ~

*T*he next few years were filled with rewarding challenges for Prad. He became the *go to* med student who could stitch up a patient with the finesse of a French couturier.

When asked where he had acquired such skills, he would say he learned them from his grandfather, a ship builder who made his own sails. While western medicine healed many, Prad often infused the holistic oils, ointments and herbs which Aloysius used to help his patients.

In what seemed like the blink of an eye, family and friends prepared to celebrate Prad's graduation. The Boyles, Mazie, Bernadette and Uncle Patrick descended upon the townhouse Prad had purchased in London. Renovations had been completed upon the section of the house Prad would use as an office. Uncle Patrick already had a list of London's elite waiting to make Dr. Pradraig Knez their physician.

Bernadette eagerly celebrated Prad's new career, but she knew that for him to be truly successful, he would need someone to oversee his house. She had already chosen the perfect individual for the job - Margaret O'Donnell.

Margaret, called Mildred by all who knew her, was from Castleogary, County Donegal. She was a trained nurse and knew all about the Knights. Her sister, Dorothy, was a bookkeeper. Together, they would guarantee that Prad's medical practice was handled professionally.

While the office portion of the house was ready for business, the remainder of the townhouse needed renovations which would make it a safe haven for the Knights. They only people who could do the work were the Knights themselves. Of course, the man in charge of that project was none other than Gerry.

Gerry was helped by Catherine and Bill's children.

The siblings, now grown and successful in their own right, had apprenticed with the tradesmen in the village just as Prad had done. Willie was an engineer with a special interest in innovative technology. He was often found puttering in Gerry's workshop. Peggy had become a legal eagle. Her mind was sharp and her use of language was only one of the weapons in her lawyer's toolbox.

Whenever Bernadette got word that the Bishop was in need of legal advice, she turned to Peggy. Jimmy was still in training, but he was able bodied and had a keen interest in security measures that could keep the Knights safe. He was quickly becoming an expert on the safest modes of travel and the best routes to reach a destination.

Gerry and the Welsh children went to London. With their help, the residence was transformed to include a state of the art laboratory behind the examining rooms. The laboratory contained the latest equipment from x-ray machines to mechanical ventilators.

Gerry was fascinated with the x-ray machine. He constantly regaled the group with stories of what he had observed during his time with Thomas Edison. Gerry could never talk about Edison without mentioning his feud with Nikolas Tesla, considered the true genius of his time.

Since this trip to London was the first for the Welsh children, they were anxious to make good use of their free time. They wanted to go everywhere and see everything but they had failed to bring disguises with them... disguises which would allow them to go out in public without attracting attention. Prad saw the sadness in the children's eyes and came up with a solution.

Rising early one morning, Prad left the house before the sun came up. By the time breakfast was being served, he was back and had surprises ready for everyone.

Waiting outside the townhouse was a private coach to take them around the city. Laid out on the dining room table were *costumes*... clothing which would allow them to blend in with regular society.

There was uniforms from a private boy's school for Willie and Jimmy and a novitiate's habit for Peggy. Gerry's mustache had, at first, been a problem, but Prad solved it by renting a coachman's outfit. Gerry would guide the carriage around town and since his seat was in the back of the coach, he would practically be invisible.

Prad had also created an itinerary for the day's excursions. First on the list – the zoo. Thinking ahead, he had visited the zoo's administrator and explained that he would be bringing a visitor who was wheelchair bound. He asked for permission to enter via the employee gate rather than general admission.

When they arrived at the zoo, Gerry climbed down off the coach and onto the wheelchair. Peggy put blankets on the seat to raise Gerry up higher and covered his legs so he would appear infirm.

Such cleverness gave everyone reason to laugh. They could not believe all that Prad had accomplished and accomplished quickly at that. He explained that being the nephew of newly appointed Judge Patrick Kane had its perks.

Their day in London was a never-to-be-forgotten event.

Gerry's eyes grew large at the sight of Big Ben. They found the changing of the guard at Buckingham Palace impressive beyond their wildest imagination. St. Paul's Cathedral and Westminster Abbey left them speechless.

As much as they enjoyed each of the stops along their itinerary, it was the time at the zoo that left the most lasting impression. Having been to the zoo so many times, Prad was able to give his friends a private tour.

He told the Welsh siblings of the fun he had had when coming to the zoo with his parents on his first visit to London. The children expressed the wish that their parents had been able to join them and promised that they would tell them everything they saw in complete detail.

Gerry loved the animals, but it was the mechanical processes that allowed the zoo to operate efficiently that held his attention. Attending to a man in a wheelchair gave the group access to closed off areas. When no one was around, Gerry got out of the chair and studied the inner workings of the zoo up close.

As a special surprise, Prad hired a photographer to meet them at the zoo. Since this was the first time so many Knights had enjoyed a day among *normal* society, he wanted to have proof of their adventure. In the photograph, five happy people are smiling their biggest smiles and waving to the camera.

Later in the day, Prad took his extended family to a restaurant. When the group realized where they would be eating, they nearly fainted.

Gerry said that even with all the clever disguises he had worn over the years, he had never come this close to common folks.

"Prad, me boy, what about the wheelchair?"

Gerry was concerned that his predicament would prevent the others from dining inside.

"Do not worry. This restaurant makes accommodations for people unable to walk. We will have a fine meal and you will be able to tell everyone how you finally ate somewhere other than The Red Hand in the Village."

"Now, that will be an interesting conversation. Let's go. I'm famished."

As the coach pulled up to the townhouse at the end of the night, what sounded like a thousand voices saying "Thank You" could be heard from inside. Prad assured his guests that nothing he could do now or in the future would repay they kindnesses shown to him. His one regret for the day was that Aloysius and Mr. and Mrs. Welsh had not been present.

"Should I not succeed as a doctor, today has proven that I would make a terrific tour guide for the Knight community."

CHAPTER TWENTY-EIGHT

"Being happy never goes out of style."
~ Lily Pulitzer ~

In the morning, Prad was awakened by the sound of hammers and drills. Wires for the electrical service were being installed. There were pipes being laid for indoor plumbing and central heating and connections for a telephone. In the midst of it all... giving orders... was Gerry.

Each day, Prad and his army of workers toiled hard, but no matter how tired they were when the sun went down, they still had energy for the evening's activities. On clear nights, they would look at the stars through a telescope Gerry had presented to Prad as a housewarming gift. The talked about the constellations and the prospects for what might lay beyond what was visible to them.

When they exhausted all ideas for the growing universe, they discussed matters closer to home. They talked about Abraham in the bible and Abraham Lincoln. Without fail, Teddy Roosevelt's name was entered into the conversation because Gerry could not go a day without praising his idol.

Once the books starting arriving, Prad's house became a replica of the village library. Mr. and Mrs. Welsh had carefully chosen literary tomes, both fiction and non-fiction. They had included reference books, how-to manuals and guide books to places around the world. There were chronicles and journals and diaries of famous people. And there were the latest medical books to aid Prad as he treated his patients. As each box was opened, Prad was awed by its content. His gratitude to the wonderful folks in the village grew by the minute.

While Prad unpacked the books and arranged them on the shelves in his office, Gerry was creating a beautiful courtyard behind the house. Prad's only request was that the garden contain a grotto where the Rosa Mystica would be the center of attention.

Mildred had a special devotion to St Therese di Lisieux, The Little Flower. She often spoke of St. Therese and how her life of simplicity and practicality had enhanced her faith. Prad rarely commented when Mildred spoke, but when the grotto was completed, he surprised Mildred by placing a statue St Therese beside that of the Rosa Mystica.

After an especially tiring day of painting, moving furniture and unpacking crates of *this and that*, the slaphappy workers began to tease each other. They began by accusing Gerry of being a slave driver, and they threatened to start a union demanding better conditions.

Gerry was unfazed. He merely asked, "What would your group of unionized workers be called?"

"I believe," Peggy said, "that we should take our inspiration from the theatrical world. "We will call ourselves *Sheriff Gerry and His Famous Trio of Dancing Cowboys.*"

Willie whooped with laughter. "Does that mean we get to wear spurs?"

"And a hat like Gerry's," Jimmy chimed in.

The kids formed a line in the middle of the living room and

began to do a jig. They danced until they could barely breathe and then fell to the floor in a fit of giggles.

Gerry shook an admonishing finger at them, but the smile on his face told a different story. Prad watched their antics without commenting. An idea was forming in his creative mind.

Two days later, a delivery man laden with boxes rang the front door bell. It took him three trips from the truck parked at the curb to get everything inside. Prad announced that he had another surprise. He had purchased a camera and all related equipment. Actually, he had bought two cameras - one was for Gerry to pull apart and put back together.

Prad informed the group that the photographer who had taken their pictures at the zoo was coming by the house to give him a lesson. He asked Gerry and the Welsh siblings to hide themselves in a place where they could see and hear everything that happened. In this way, they would be just as knowledgeable as Prad and could take the equipment with them when they returned to Glenties.

With a somewhat sad look on his face, Prad told Willie, Peggy and Jimmy to be certain to take lots of pictures with their parents. This was one of Prad's biggest regrets. He had none with Stjephan and Vesna.

When the photographer arrived, he set up one camera in front of the couch. Then, he instructed Prad on how to pose his subjects and adjust the lenses and lighting. He gave detailed advice on the best times of day to take pictures and what was needed to develop the film.

Gerry and the Welsh children listened attentively from their hiding place. As soon as he was gone, they tumbled out of the walls and talked non stop of all they had learned.

As the group carefully examined the camera equipment, Prad slipped quietly from the room. When he returned, he was carrying boxes with the Harrod's logo on the cover. In a solemn voice, he announced that Christmas had come early.

The camera lost its appeal as Prad began calling out their

names one by one. Inside the boxes were cowboy hats, denim pants, cowboy boots, spurs and neckerchiefs. There was even a set of everything for Mildred who, Prad said, would be the group's medic.

When all the gifts had been given out except one, Prad motioned for Gerry to come close. Gerry opened the box Prad handed to him in a solemn manner and, suddenly, began to laugh from deep in his belly. He held the gift up for the kids to see. It was a sheriff's badge. *Sheriff Gerry and his Trio of Dancing Cowboys* were ready for business.

Peggy, Willie and Jimmy ran off to change into their costumes. Since Gerry's regular attire was the basis for the clothing Prad had bought, all he had to do was put on the badge.

When the kids returned, Gerry teased, "I sure hope I do not look as ridiculous as each of you."

Using the suggestions the photographer had given him, Prad arranged the group into a charming pose. He snapped a few pictures... enough so that Mr. and Mrs. Welsh would have photos of each of their children and a group shot to put into their frames.

Prad convinced Gerry to pose alone by saying that the photo would be needed when he received the Sheriff of the Year award. The kids then convinced Prad and Gerry to have a picture taken together. This photo was the one destined to be cherished forever.

CHAPTER TWENTY-NINE

"A man's growth is seen in the successive choirs of his friends."
~ Ralph Waldo Emerson~

The construction on the townhouse was almost complete when Mazie showed up for a surprise visit. She was thrilled to see Gerry and the younger Welshes. They talked for over an hour, catching up on what had been happening in Glenties and the Village.

Peggy, Willie and Jimmy took turns telling Mazie about their exploring London, dinner in a "real" restaurant and, of course, the photographs that had been taken. When Prad got home and saw Mazie, he wrapped her in his arms. She was one of his favorite people and, while he was thrilled by her visit, he knew she had come for a special reason.

Arm in arm, Prad and Mazie went out into the beautiful new garden which Gerry had created. They sat in front of the grotto and held hands as only good friends can do. Mazie told Prad that she had met someone special. She was in love. His name was

Joseph Maguire and he was from Frosses, a small village not far from Glenties. Prad expressed his absolute delight in her good fortune.

Quizzically, he asked, "Isn't Frosses the place where one side of the village doesn't talk to the other?"

Mazie raised her eyebrows in response. "Yes, Prad, because one side of the village is a cemetery."

When their laughter subsided, Mazie told Prad all there was to know about Joe. He was a few years older than she. With the help of Bishop O'Donnell, he had earned a law degree from University of Dublin. The company he worked for specialized in representing companies in the coal mining industry.

Two years ago, while he was in France seeing a client, the Courrières' mine disaster happened. Joe had helped with the rescue efforts. His lungs were damaged and, ever since, he has suffered with recurring health issues.

Prad was both concerned and impressed. Courrières was one of the worst mining disasters in recorded history.

While coal mining was not a major industry in France, there were still a number of mines in operation. Over 1000 miners perished in the Courrières disaster. No reason had been found for the coal dust explosion, fingers were pointed in all directions, lawsuits had been filed and politicians had, not surprisingly, gotten involved.

Prad knew the survivors and rescuers had ongoing health problems. Joe was a brave man to have pitched in and helped with the rescue efforts.

Mazie explained that while their physician, Dr. Adair, was a dear sweet man, he was not Prad. She hoped that Prad would be willing to examine Joe's lungs by taking x-rays and doing whatever other tests were needed.

Mazie had every intention of marrying Joe, despite his health problems. Joe, however, would not agree to marriage if he was going to be a burden to his wife.

Immediate arrangements were made for Joe to come to

London. Prad explained that major strides were being made in the treatment of lung disease. He could not guarantee a cure, but he assured her that the only thing she needed to worry about was the guest list for her wedding.

Joe Maguire arrived at the townhouse just as the finishing touches were being added to the renovations. He was a fine fellow and Prad could see why Mazie was smitten.

X-rays were taken and together Joe and Prad studied the images. Prad pointed to areas where the mine gasses had damaged the lungs. The damage was consistent with research Prad and other doctors had been doing in recent years. This research had resulted in new medicine protocols that had proven promising.

Joe waited expectantly for advice on how to proceed with his treatment. Little did he expect to be told to "... go fly a kite." Prad may have been on the cutting edge of new protocols but being told to fly a kite was bizarre.

To answer the questions in Joe's eyes, Prad said, "Take these pills as prescribed. Go home to Donegal. Go to the ocean and spend your days flying a kite high over the waters. The salt air will do wonders for you."

Six months later, Prad arrived in Glenties to attend Joe's and Mazie's wedding.

And a beautiful wedding it was... except for the attendance of one guest - Barbraella. Prad had seen the young woman a handful of times over the years, but he had never gone out of his way to spend time with her.

As was dictated by society, he said "Hello" and inquired about her health. She proudly announced that she was betrothed to an Australian by the name of Nicholas Bitters. She shared with Prad that Nicholas came from a well-to-do family that owned sheep and cattle ranches. He had been educated in England and, like Prad, had graduated from Oxford.

Prad asked to be introduced to Barbraella's new found love as he would enjoy meeting a fellow Oxonian. Nicholas, unfortunately, was attending to business matters in London. London was where she and Nicholas planned to live once they were married.

"Perhaps," she said, "we will be neighbors."

Prad was rescued from answering when he heard Bernadette calling him.

"What did that girl want with you?" Daggers shot from Bernadette's eyes.

Prad was taken aback by the tone of Bernadette's voice. He knew she loved all of God's children, but none of that love was evident in the way she said Barbraella's name.

Realizing how unchristian she sounded, Bernadette raised her eyes to the heavens and said, "Pay me no mind, Prad. I am Irish and Catholic. I am filled with guilt for having a loose tongue and, because there is no beer in heaven, I have had far too much of it today, which is the reason for my loose tongue."

Prad and Bernadette doubled over with laughter.

In the middle of Bernadette's explanation, Barbraella appeared again and inquired at the cause of their hilarity.

"I was telling Prad about a funny sermon I heard while attending a Sunday service," Bernadette said.

Barbraella stared Bernadette in the face and challenged her. "Bernadette, I feel as though you have never liked me."

Bernadette denied any such feeling. "Not true, *cailin*. Those thoughts are all your own."

"Deny all you want, Bernadette, but I know better. Some people say I am a mean person. It is not true."

Barbraella paused for a moment and a smirk appeared on her face. "I have the heart of a sweet girl... in my closet, in a jar."

Bernadette and Prad were struck dumb. They watched as Barbraella flounced off, head held high and shoulders held stiffly.

CHAPTER THIRTY

"An old trick well done is far better than a new trick with no effect"
~ Harry Houdini ~

*E*arly on in his practice, Prad received an unusual request. He was asked to go to the Oxford Music Hall late one evening. When he arrived, a show was ending and waiting in the wings for him was none other than the great magician Harry Houdini. Prad was dumbfounded.

"Dr. Knez, kako si?" Houdini addressed Prad in Croatian, asking how he was doing.

Prad responded, "Dobro sam. Zadovoljstvo mi je upoznati vas."

Houdini, having been born in Hungary, was fluent in Croatian. The two countries were practically conjoined twins.

Houdini continued the conversation in English, "I am glad you are well. It is a pleasure to make your acquaintance. I recently met your Uncle... Judge Kane. He spoke highly of you. However, he failed to tell me your age. You are quite young to be a doctor."

Prad explained that people were always surprised and a little hesitant to allow treatment when they first met him. They quickly changed their minds when they realized how well he was trained and the extent of his knowledge. If Houdini wanted someone older, he would understand.

Houdini shook his head to indicate that Prad's age was not an issue. He needed someone who was discreet and Prad assured him that confidentiality was of utmost importance where his patients were concerned.

Convinced that he had found the right physician for his needs, Houdini admitted to Prad that he feared the injuries he had sustained during his career were taking a toll on him physically and emotionally. He was plagued by anxiety. An appointment was scheduled for the next day.

Mildred was informed that a new patient would be arriving in the morning. She was advised to use utmost discretion when meeting him. Prad scheduled x-rays and a battery of tests.

Dr. Leopold Weiss, Houdini's brother, was a New York based radiologist. According to Houdini, his brother was well-informed on the workings of the machine. He jokingly told Prad that his brother had used him as a "test subject" when perfecting his technique.

Houdini was surprisingly fit. While people did not normally expect a person who made their living as a magician/illusionist to be athletic, Houdini was strong and muscular. Prad acknowledged that he was happy a comparison of his own muscles was not needed to prove he was a good diagnostician.

Despite his obvious strength and strong build, Houdini's body showed signs of wear and tear. Prad advised him to consider leaving certain stunts out of his routine for a while. Houdini laughed, knowing he would never disappoint his audiences by denying them his most death-defying magic tricks.

For the anxiety, Prad recommended lavender oil, which, he knew from experience, had a sedative-like effect. Houdini was advised to apply the oil only at night to assure him a better night's sleep. Should unexpected visitors comment on the flowery scent, Houdini could claim it was his wife's perfume.

Houdini was impressed with the renovations that had been made to the townhouse and asked for a tour of the living quarters. Prad agreed, taking him into the parlor and lower level areas. Houdini studied the rooms carefully, focusing on the placement of the walls and certain pieces of built-in furniture.

"My dear young man," he said to Prad, "you have secrets."

Houdini walked to one of the bookcases and felt along the surface of the casing. The bookcase moved. Prad jolted forward, attempting to stop the bookcase from opening.

"Do not fear, Prad. You are keeping my secrets, and I, in turn, will keep yours. I am curious, however, why you need secret passages in this old house."

Prad felt forced to explain. He told Houdini about the Knights, especially Gerry and Willie. When Houdini heard of Gerry's expertise with trap doors, he became fascinated and asked to meet him.

Prad promised to introduce them the next time Gerry came to town. In the meantime, he could meet Willie, who was expected within a week. Willie was working on a project requiring research that could only be found at Oxford. Houdini excitedly set a date and time.

As he was about to leave, Houdini commented that few people would be as accepting of the Knights as was Prad. He recognized that Prad was non-judgmental and able to see beyond the physical appearance of those he met. He asked if Prad enjoyed going to the circus and explained that circus performers were among his closest friends.

"They need a doctor who does not see them as freaks. They need someone who will treat them no differently than anyone else."

Prad understood and assured Houdini that, should he send his friends to him for medical care, he would treat them with the same consideration he gave to Gerry, Aloysius and the other Knights.

Mildred and Prad discussed Houdini's visit at the end of the day. Should circus performers become patients, Prad would need to schedule their appointments at a time when the office was least busy.

"Your uncle and his friends might not take as kindly to their presence as you do, Prad. You do not want to do more harm than good."

Prad realized how lucky he was to have Mildred to help him.

Houdini was good to his word. Soon, the people who thrilled audiences by flying high over the center ring of the Big Top and those who brought laughter on the ground were calling for appointments.

Prad treated them with respect, kindness and understanding. Their ailments were the same as all people with health issues – heart palpitations, ingrown toenails, boils and, sadly, an abuse of alcohol. The Bearded Lady did pose a special problem as she was concerned her hair was falling out and her career was dependent on remaining hirsute.

Mildred enjoyed their visits. She would chat with them, sharing stories from her own life. One day, she took the high wire walker and the clown who was shot out of a cannon into the garden to show them the grotto. She explained why the statues of Rosa Mystica and St. Therese were important.

The clown was especially touched by Mildred's devotion and said he would pray to the ladies before every performance in the hope that they would keep him safe.

As planned, Willie arrived the following week and Gerry came with him.

When the two men appeared from behind the bookcase, Houdini was waiting to greet them. By way of explanation, Houdini said, "We each have societies that are best kept secret from the rest of the world."

Gerry and Willie, of course, knew that Houdini was the master of illusion. He was, in a sense, their idol. The three men talked for hours.

Gerry half jokingly said that installing the lock on the front door of the townhouse was the first time he had ever needed to secure a premises from intruders. He explained that no locks were used in the Knights' Village.

"A lock was as strange to me as illusions are to your audiences. I have always enjoyed the mechanics of how something works, especially things like your boxes with fake bottoms and hidden compartments. Before installing the lock on the door, I spent weeks taking it apart and putting it back together. Now, Willie here is learning the tricks of the trade."

Houdini showed Gerry, Willie and Prad the breathing exercises he did to perform his stunts. Controlling his breathing, he explained, was tantamount to staying alive when confined to a small space. He told them how he had practiced by submerging his younger self in an oversized bathtub filled to the brim with water. Sometimes, he would add ice to strengthen his endurance.

Gerry inquired how Houdini knew that the house had hidden passages, and Houdini confessed that in examining the woodwork, he had seen a flaw in what was otherwise master craftsmanship. Only when he realized the flaw was intentional did he understand there was more to the house than met the eye.

As the morning progressed, the conversation moved from magic to the reason for Willie's and Gerry's visit. Willie said he had come to London to study submarines. He and Gerry were trying to keep up with the latest technology.

Houdini mentioned that airplanes piqued his interest, which led to Gerry telling him about the Shamrock Express.

"Prad can weave a basket as well as anyone I know, and he is an expert at choosing the proper fabrics for the balloons. All my boys are well trained."

Houdini checked his watch and stood to leave. "My wife is expecting me to spend the day with her."

He expressed his delight in meeting Gerry and Willie and said he looked forward to more meetings in the future.

Willie watched Houdini as he walked away. "Prad, my boy, your house is magical in so many ways

CHAPTER THIRTY-ONE

"If you remain calm in the midst of great chaos, it is the surest
guarantee that it will eventually subside."
~ Julie Andrews ~

*U*nexpectedly, Prad was forced to face one of those *matters of life* of which Gerry had warned him. He needed to visit the Dingle Peninsula where his parents had perished and say his final goodbyes.

He wrote to Bernadette, Gerry and the Boyles, telling them of his plans. They all offered to go with him, but Prad felt this was something he needed to do alone. He would stay with the Boyles, his surrogate family, while he was in Ireland.

The Boyles house was filled with memories – happy and sad – which flooded over Prad as he stood on the front lawn. He missed his parents and was angry with the way they had perished. He hated the sea serpent for taking them from him. Being with the people he loved and who loved him would, hopefully, allow his heart and soul to heal.

When Prad arrived at Glenties, Owen and Juliana were in Belfast on business but Joe and Mazie were home. The reunion was short but happy even with the specter of what lay ahead foremost in Prad's mind.

In the early morning hours before the sun burned away the morning mist, Prad prepared for the day ahead. Bernadette was awake and waiting for him in the kitchen. Food for his journey had been prepared and there was a satchel with a change of clothes.

The journey from Glenties to the Dingle Peninsula took five hours. The Earl of Cork's house has been readied for him, no doubt thanks to Bernadette and the Knights. Prad was tired when he arrived and decided to wait until morning to visit the place where he had last seen his parents.

Morning found Prad sitting on the still wet sand, trying to block the more graphic visual images of his parents death. He could not stop the pictures that flooded his memory... the serpent rising from the waters, its fangs tearing into his parents, the boat shattering like so many toothpicks floating in the waves.

He felt again the serpent's tail whipping him and lifting him high into the air. He felt oxygen forced from his lungs and the water closing over his head as he sank below the ocean's surface. He remembered the life draining from his body at the same moment he felt fresh air fill his nose and throat.

Prad closed his eyes and saw the strange image of a person - a half person/half fish holding his head above the water and pulling him to safety. He felt the hard, cold surface of stone under his back. He was in a cave but how he got there, he did not know.

Prad had forgotten that if not for this... this... whatever he was, he would not be sitting on the wet sand in the cold morning mist reliving that day over and over again. Was his mind playing tricks on him? Did his brush with death take him to a place unknown to mankind?

What was real? What was imagined? He needed to know, and yet, he did not want to know for knowing would make the pain of losing his parents more intense.

Slowly, he stood up and brushed the wet sand off his pants, cursing himself for not remembering to sit on one of the blankets stored in his knapsack. He surveyed his surroundings. A cave could be seen in a nearby outcropping. Was this the cave where he had been taken on that fateful day? Was it from there that he had stepped out into a painful reality upon hearing Owen Boyle calling his name?

Hesitantly, Prad walked to the opening in the rocks and entered the all-consuming darkness. Shadows surrounded him. One of those shadows appeared to have arms.

Upon closer inspection, Prad saw that it was the tweed jacket he had been wearing when the serpent threw him into the water. Prad touched the fabric. The jacket was still smooth and soft and, surprisingly, dry. He lifted it to his nose, expecting to smell mildew. There was only the scent of the sea.

Prad put the jacket over his arm, intending to take it with him. He felt something fall out of the pocket and hit his leg. On the ground at his feet, was the cap Bernadette had given him... the cap embroidered with his name – Pádraig. Tears began to wet his cheeks. He picked up the cap and buried his face in it. He cried tears that had been waiting to be shed for a very long time.

Time passed. The walls of the cave no longer echoed with his sobs. Prad dried his eyes and composed himself. With great effort, he turned to the opening in the rocks, planning to return to the beach.

No sooner did he step into the sunlight than he saw his nemesis attacking a young woman who had been collecting shells near the water's edge. Prad dropped his jacket and cap.

The serpent held the screaming woman in its mouth. It tossed her about just as it had Prad's parents. Helplessness washed over Prad. He wanted to save her. He needed to save her... but how.

As if in answer to a prayer, a trident fell from the sky, landing next to him. Moving on instinct, he picked up the weapon and hurled it at the beast with all the strength in his body. The trident sailed like a guided missile and found its target in the serpent's eye.

Feeling some of the pain it had caused others, the serpent spit the woman into the sea and sank below the water. Prad ran to the beach. He felt no sympathy for the creature. His only intent was to help the injured woman.

What he saw when he reached the water's edge would change his life forever. A man… a half-man… was struggling to save the half-woman beside him. They were both seriously injured, but their only interest was securing a large pear whelk. Prad ran faster, intending to offer assistance in getting the whelk to safety.

"Mermaids! Mermen! Am I really seeing what I think I see." Prad muttered aloud the thoughts that were flooding his practical mind. "Grief is driving me crazy."

The Merman turned to Prad; his eyes filled with fear. He had a large gash down his back from his neck to his fin. The Mermaid appeared to be unconscious. Prad realized that the Merman was trying to save both the female and whelk, which he now saw held a baby.

Prad yelled, "Do not move. I will help you."

The Merman froze. Prad got closer and gently turned the Merman so he could examine his wound. "Please. Stay very still while I look after your family."

The Mermaid's injuries were life threatening. Prad's heart broke as he knew her chances for survival were slim.

Ever so gently, Prad moved the Mermaid to a more secure section of the beach. He returned for the Merman and helped him move so he could be with his wife. Prad had no doubt that these three were a family. He saw the pain in the Merman's eyes.

He also saw the same depth of love his parents had felt for each other. There was tenderness in Prad's touch as he lifted the pear whelk and placed it in the Merman's arms.

Prad saw the Merman shiver which caused him to remember the blankets he had in his knapsack.

"I will be right back."

CHAPTER THIRTY-TWO

"The test of a civilization is in the way that it cares for its helpless members."
~ Pearl S. Buck ~

When he returned with the blankets, Prad covered the Merman and the baby. Then, he turned to the Mermaid. He gently propped her head up with a mound of soft seagrass and covered her with another blanket.

Prad and the Merman looked at each other, and Prad saw the unspoken plea in the Merman's eyes.

Prad said, "I will try."

Engaging all of his skills and his vast knowledge of medicine, Prad examined the Mermaid's body. He moved her hair from her face and was momentarily stunned by her beauty. She was pale with what he knew to be a faux flush of color in her cheeks. Her body was struggling against the odds. He knew he had to work quickly if she was to survive.

Prad put his ear to her chest. Her breathing was shallow. He opened her mouth and cleared her airway as best he could. She was growing weaker by the minute.

The Mermaid's injuries and the recent birth of the baby had taken a toll on her body. He doubted she was strong enough to recover but he would not stop trying.

Prad was glad that he thought to move the threesome close to one another. Should the Mermaid awaken from her unconscious state, she would know her husband and child were with her.

He advised the Merman, "Talk to her. I believe she can hear you. Encourage her to fight. While the odds are against her, she is showing signs of improvement."

The Merman, though seriously injured and in pain, talked to his wife and daughter. He moved his head from one to the other, taking in every detail of their faces. Prad heard the tender words which the Merman whispered... words which revealed the love this man felt for his family. He was surprised to hear the Merman say that he trusted "... this human."

With what little strength he had, the Merman threw off the blanket that was covering his lower half, revealing that his fin had turned to legs. He lifted the blanket covering his wife, revealing that she, too, had changed. Prad was struck dumb by what he was seeing.

His wonderment ceased when he heard the female moaning. Under the blanket, she was covered in blood.

The man tried to stand while pleading, "Please. Do not let her die!"

His legs could not hold his weight and he fell, reopening his wounds. Blood was everywhere.

Prad moved the man a short distance away so he could attend to each patient without obstruction. He put pressure on the Merman's cut, which slowed the bleeding. By the time he got back to the female, she had passed. No words were needed to tell the husband that his wife had died. The slump of Prad's shoulders and his sobs of distress said it all.

With help from Prad, the man crawled over to the woman and

rested his head on her chest. He cried enough tears to refill the ocean had it gone dry. Prad was concerned that the agony the man was feeling would cause him to die as well. A broken heart was not merely an expression. The pain of losing a loved one was very real.

Prad gently touched the Merman's shoulder and said, "Your daughter needs you now. You cannot allow yourself to perish with grief. Come. I must attend to your injuries before infection sets in."

The laceration in the man's back needed suturing to stop the bleeding, but Prad had no instruments with which to complete the task. The sound of a bird's wings flapping close to his head forced Prad to look skyward. A puffin hovered within finger's touch. The bird dropped a fishing hook with line attached onto the beach.

The Merman called out the bird's name, "Argyle."

The bird swooped in close to the man as if to say, "I am here." Then, it was gone. Prad had once again seen what he thought to be a miracle... a bird had provided a solution to a medical emergency and the man and the bird were friends.

Prad knew there was no time to waste. He needed to work quickly and efficiently. He cleaned the hook and line as best he could while explaining to the man that the stitching process would cause a great deal of pain. Taking a deep breath, Prad pierced the man's body with the hook and began to expertly place his sutures. The man cried out and fainted... a blessing if ever there was one.

In desperation, Prad gathered long strands of seaweed with which to make a bandage. The salt water in which the seaweed had grown would help prevent an infection.

With the man out of immediate danger, Prad checked on the baby, who he saw was a girl. He picked up the whelk and, for just a moment, looked upon this child who was oblivious to all that had happened.

"Another miracle," Prad said aloud.

Still holding the pear whelk, Prad returned to his patient. Another shock awaited him. The salt water had turned the man's legs back into a beautiful long tail and fin.

Prad put the baby down next to its father. "Your daddy is here, little one," Prad said. Then, turned away so he could cry.

His sorrows spent, Prad decided to bring the Mermaid to where her husband and daughter rested. He carried her ever so gently and placed her on the ground. The baby in the whelk he put between her mother and father.

A sound from beyond their hiding place echoed in the silence. Prad could not decide if it was a cry of distress or a warning that danger was approaching. Stepping out into the open, he saw Argyle struggling to control his avian emotions. If birds could cry for the loss of a loved one, this puffin was truly in agony.

Argyle was perched on a small flat ledge that jutted out from a sand dune. The ledge resembled a landing strip and allowed the puffin to come and go with ease. Prad sat next to him.

Argyle did not shy away. Rather, he moved closed to Prad and rested his head on Prad's shoulder. Together, man and animal mourned the loss of life. Argyle cried for his friends – Glenn, Muriel and their daughter.

Prad cried for many reasons... for his inability to save the Mermaid's life, for the child who had lost her mother, for the husband who had lost his wife and for the realization that no matter how good a doctor he may have been, he was not God and could not change destiny.

Time passed. Argyle began poking Prad with his beak. Prad stirred from the emotional cellar where he had taken refuge. He heard the baby crying.

Sharing a look of emotional devastation with his feathered companion, he stood up and placed a gentle hand on the puffin's head. Argyle rubbed against Prad's palm in shared friendship. With stooped shoulders, Prad walked to where the baby and her parents lay hidden. He picked her up and held her close in his arms.

The mangle of thick, strappy phormiums, pittosporum and bindweed was a fortress that would keep her safe temporarily, but she would need someone to care for her who was strong and healthy... someone able to defend her against potential enemies.

The mist coming in off the ocean gave Prad a chill. He took the baby and walked along the beach, allowing the sun to warm them both. Walking seemed to soothe the baby so Prad continued along the beach until he could hear soft snores from the contented child. Then, he returned to the hiding place, ready to put her back in her whelk.

The fortress was empty. The Merman and the Mermaid were gone. The pearl whelk lay where Prad had placed it between the baby's parents, the blankets Prad had used to cover them were on the ground as was the fish hook that Prad had used to stitch the male's wounds. All else remained undisturbed.

Prad laid the baby in the whelk and ran back to the beach. He scoured the coastline looking for signs that the Merman and Mermaid were nearby. The waters were calm and still. Not even a ripple disturbed the peacefulness of the scene before him. If not for the baby, Prad would have thought the events of the day had been a dream.

CHAPTER THIRTY-THREE

"All things are difficult before they are easy."
~ Thomas Fuller ~

*T*he Earl's house was quiet when Prad unlocked the front door. He took the little girl into the spare room, laid her on the bed and unwrapped the blanket in which she had been swaddled. She was a beautiful child, her features exquisite in every detail. She was also a happy child. She cooed and gurgled, leaving a trail of little bubbles on her lips.

Prad accepted that he had been entrusted with a gift from the heavens. He examined the baby from head to toe and declared her *perfect*.

Once the baby fell asleep and he finally had a minute for himself, Prad went to the dry sink to pour himself a drink. He had one particular alcoholic beverage in mind – Usquaebach - Gaelic for *the water of life*. Uncorking the bottle, Prad thought that there had never been a more fitting time to partake of this liquor. He poured himself a healthy dose, then sat down to ponder his next course of action.

"I must return to Glenties and I must do it quickly. Bernadette and Mazie will know how to care for the baby properly," he said aloud.

With no one there to provide feedback, he picked up the phone and dialed a number he knew by heart. Bernadette answered. After relaying the story of the Merman, Mermaid and Merbaby, he asked Bernadette if Gerry was available. An emergency trip to the Dingle Peninsula aboard the Shamrock Express was required.

Prad estimated the time it would take for Gerry to make landing on the beach. He was waiting when Gerry hopped out of the basket and ran to Prad.

"Let me see! Let me see! Where is she, lad?"

Prad retrieved the pear whelk from behind a bramble bush. He lowered the blanket so Gerry could see what was inside.

"Jesus, Mary and the other guy." was his awed response.

Within minutes, two men and a baby were rising above the land. The Shamrock Express was headed back to Glenties.

"What is her name? Do you even know?"

"No. I don't know her name, but her mother's name was Muriel. Watch out for the puffin!"

"What, in God's name, are you talking about... puffin?"

"Overhead. His name is Argyle. I will explain how I know that when we get back to Glenties."

The rest of the trip was quiet as the two men stood watch over the angel in the shell. This angel had no wings. A beautiful iridescent sea green tailfin took their place.

As the Shamrock Express rose higher and higher into the clouds, Irwin and Proteus searched the solid ground below for their granddaughter. They saw the balloon but paid little attention to it. At any other time, they would have been curious. This day, they were on a mission.

After an exhaustive few hours, the grandfathers and those who had joined in the search returned to Wading River. Neither man looked forward to telling his wife or Glenn of their failure to find the child.

Glenn was staying with his parents while he recovered from his wounds. He was mostly unconscious, occasionally awakening to mutter his wife's name and call for his daughter.

As the search party came into sight, Mirasol and Salacia swam out to meet them. The look on their husband's faces foretold their lack of success. The women fell into their husband's arms and wept.

Glenn's well-being was of concern to both his father and father-in-law. They asked about his recovery and were relieved that, while he was not improved, neither had his condition deteriorated.

Irwyn and Mirasol took their leave, saying they had matters to attend to at home. Salacia understood the pain Mirasol and Irwyn were feeling, returning to the house where their daughter had grown up and where now they must prepare for a funeral. She kissed Mirasol and held her close. No words were needed.

As time passed, Glenn's condition began to improve. Within days, he was conscious and alert. One look at his parents' faces and he knew that the nightmares he had been experiencing were memories that he wanted to block from his mind.

He feared asking about his daughter and shuddered at being told she had been taken by a human. When he learned the man was someone who had been on the beach the day of the attack, Glenn's anxiety was somewhat relieved. He remembered the man who had helped them. He remembered how that man had tried to save Muriel and how he had cared for Glenn's injuries. Perhaps, his daughter was safe after all.

With a heavy heart, Glenn asked about the funeral arrangements for Muriel. Proteus and Salacia explained that Irwyn and Salacia had waited, wanting Glenn to have an opportunity to say a final goodbye. Only Nautilus' permission was needed for Glenn to move about.

And so it was that Proteus informed Irwyn and Mirasol of Glenn's recovery and his appreciation that they had waited for him before burying Muriel. The next day would be the hardest of their lives.

CHAPTER THIRTY-FOUR

"May the saddest day of your future be no worse than the happiest
day of your past."
~ Irish Proverb ~

he Shamrock Express glided into Glenties. Its passengers could see Bernadette and Mazie waiting with the horse and buggy. Once the balloon touched ground, Gerry hopped out of the basket, and Prad handed him the pear whelk. Prad followed quickly behind and retrieved the baby from Gerry's adoring hands. The baby had already taken a hold of his heart.

Being moved from Prad's arms to Gerry's arms and back to Prad's arms awakened the sleeping infant.

Mazie heard her cry and ran to see "What in heaven's name is making that sound."

She looked into the shell.

"A baby! Prad, you have never even brought home a puppy, and now you bring a baby!"

Bernadette hurried everyone to the carriage, saying that all questions would be answered at home. For now, getting the baby to safety was their only priority.

Once at the Boyles' house, Bernadette and Mazie took the little girl inside while Prad brought the horse and buggy into the barn. Never before had Prad accomplished this task so quickly.

Just as everyone was settling into the living room, Joe arrived unexpectedly. He was surprised to see Prad as Mazie had told him Prad was visiting the Dingle Peninsula to memorialize his parents. Joe saw the pear whelk on the floor and heard the cooing coming from inside.

"A baby? Whose baby are we watching for the weekend?"

An uncomfortable silence followed.

Prad took the lead, explaining how he had been walking on the beach and had come upon the cave where he was taken after the accident. At the back of the cave, he found the blazer. He was exploring the deeper inside when he heard a hiss that made his heart stop beating.

Tripping over the uneven ground, he ran outside and saw the serpent – the serpent that had killed his parents – with a woman in its mouth. The woman was holding a very large sea shell.

Prad was about to scream when a different sound drew his attention. A puffin flew directly at him and dropped a trident at his feet. The bird screamed as if to tell Prad to pick it up and throw it at the serpent.

Prad did just that, penetrating one of the serpent's eyes. The shock of the stabbing forced the serpent to spit the woman and the shell into the sea. The serpent thrashed with pain and disappeared under the water.

Only then did Prad see a man... a man with a tail. He realized these people were not human; they were merfolk. Both the Merman and the Mermaid were injured and both were clinging desperately to the shell. Prad heard a cry, but this time it was not the puffin. A baby... a baby was in the shell.

The Merman saw Prad and became frightened. He immediately

attempted to draw his family away to a safer place. Humans were dangerous. Humans could hurt Merfolk.

Prad spoke softly, reassuring the Merman that he wanted to help. He could see the deep gash on the Merman's back and he realized that the Mermaid's injuries were life threatening. He knew in his heart he could not save her, but his oath to *treat the ill to the best of one's abilities* was sacred to him.

Moving slowly so as not to frighten the man even more, Prad reached his side and helped to move him and, eventually, his wife and baby, to a safe place on the beach. He cried as he told Joe how, even with using all of his medical skills, he could not save the Mermaid. Before she passed, Prad was privileged to see all of their tails – the Merman's, Mermaid's and the baby's – become human legs.

Prad took his time telling the group about Argyle. He told them about the fish hook and thread and the bird's abilities to communicate with the Merman. Prad was still amazed by the friendship between the man and the bird and now between himself and the bird.

No detail of the day was left unsaid. When Prad got to the part where he returned to the hiding place and found the Merman and Mermaid gone, Gerry, Mazie and Joe knew everything. Prad had connected all the story parts and brought them to this one moment in the living room at Glenties.

Mouths hung open. No one seemed to be breathing. They knew Prad had not kissed the Blarney Stone. This story was real.

Joe stood up and walked to the bar. He poured a drink for himself and Prad. Gerry, Mazie and Bernadette declined the offer.

"What should we do now?" Mazie directed her question to Bernadette, who was now holding the baby in her arms and rocking her back and forth.

Bernadette's answer surprised everyone. "I am going to the boathouse. It is time for a swim."

At the boathouse, Bernadette asked Joe and Prad to lower a coracle into the water, get it wet and, then, bring it inside where no one would see them. Coracle would serve as a makeshift bathtub or bathing pool.

"We must allow this child to return to her natural self from time to time."

Ever so gently, Bernadette lowered the little girl in the water. She did not hold her above the water's surface. Within minutes, the baby's legs began to disappear and her tail returned.

"We need never worry about her drowning. The sea is her natural environment. She can breathe both below the water and above."

Prad looked to the sky but Argyle was nowhere to be seen. Bernadette wrapped the baby in a big towel and carried her to the grotto. Everyone followed and, together, they bowed their heads in prayer.

Bernadette made the sign of the cross on the baby's head, much as was done during a baptism. She held the baby high for all to see and announced that from that moment on her name would be Rosa Mystica... or Mysti to those who already loved her.

EPILOGUE

"May the road rise up to meet you.
May the wind be always at your back.
May the sun shine warm upon your face,
The rains fall soft upon your fields,
And, until we meet again,
May God hold you in the palm of his hand."
~ Irish Blessing ~

*T*here was sadness in the valley.

The time came for the residents of Wading River and Muriel's immediate family to say "Goodbye." In the tradition of Merfolk, everyone traveled away from the village to the sacred place where Mermen and Mermaids were laid to rest.

Nereo, the elder who had married Glenn and Muriel, offered prayers for Muriel and for her loved ones who would mourn her passing. Even in death, Muriel's beauty had not faded. She looked peaceful, which helped to ease her parents' suffering.

Tradition held that as the deceased lay in peaceful repose, the villagers said their farewells under the watchful eye of Nereo, who led the ceremony. When all the villagers' wishes for a safe journey to the next plain of existence had been expressed, Irwyn, Mirasol, Proteus, Salacia and Glenn had their moments with Muriel.

The final ceremony was the covering of the departed with shells. At first, the mound was large and the shells plentiful. In time, the sea water would hasten the body's decomposition until all that was left were the shells.

Nereo hugged Irwyn, Mirasol, Proteus, Salacia and Glenn in turn. He choked on his own tears, making it difficult for him to speak. Shaking hands with the assembled crowd, he spoke of the existence of good and evil in the world. He reminisced, reminding everyone of the joy they had felt at Glenn's and Muriel's wedding and the news that a baby was on the way.

When Nereo spoke of the devastating news surrounding Rylee's disappearance and Muriel's passing, he advised the villagers not to allow despair to enter their lives.

"Sadness is followed by joy. Evil by good. Time does heal all wounds as evidenced by Glenn's recovery. One day soon, the pain we are all feeling will turn to something less sharp. It will be replaced by a different feeling... one of hope. You have come together for a common cause and that togetherness will lead you to a better day."

As Nereo spoke, a pod of dolphins slowly circled them. Next came the seahorses and beyond them, the whales. An abundance of sea life showed its respect in a display that had never been seen before.

At the last moment, a flash of red pierced the water. It lasted but a minute and was gone. Argyle had had bid Muriel adieu.

Glenn kissed his wife tenderly, expressing his undying love for her. He promised he would find their daughter. Tears on his face, he swam away.

Proteus and Salacia next bid their daughter-in-law farewell. Last came Irwyn and Mirasol, whose pain at losing their daughter could not be hidden. They, too, told her their love would last forever. Irwyn promised he would help to find Rylee. With one last kiss, mother and father swam away; the villagers followed them. The elders then covered Muriel in shells.

As time passed, Glenn's health improved. Every morning, he swam to Muriel's resting place and spent time talking to her.

One day, he decided to take a different route. On the ocean floor, he saw a statue of a woman covered heavily in barnacles. As he knew the ocean's floor better than anyone, he was surprised by this discovery. He decided to take a closer look.

The face of the statue was beautiful. Looking at her, Glenn felt a peacefulness settle on him. She drew him in, making him feel that he could talk to her... confide in her.

Glenn began to brush some of the looser barnacles away from the base of the statue. He noticed writing on the base of the pedestal. Most of the letters were obscured, washed away by the currents and the salt water. Glenn saw an R and letters that appeared to spell Mysti.

As if prompted from beyond, Glenn spoke to the concrete lady.

"Mysti, please tend to my wife's resting place and help me to locate my daughter. I will be your devoted servant."

From that day forward, he visited the statue every day and made the same request of her.

Glenn was returning to his former self. He felt strong; able to swim faster and for longer distances. The only noticeable after effect of the serpent's attack was what a human might call a limp in the way he moved his tail.

Knowing it would soon be time for him to go in search of Rylee, he decided to visit the cave where he and Muriel had shared special times.

As he got closer to the entrance, his heart pounded harder. Tears welled up in his eyes and blocked his throat. He started to weep.

In the dark of the cave, two eyes looked out at him. The eyes were familiar to Glenn.

"Argyle, my friend. You never leave me." Glenn choked back his tears.

Argyle bobbed his head, turned and flew deeper into the cave. When he returned, he carried a tweed cap in his beak.

"A thoughtful gesture, Argyle, but what can a man who lives in the sea do with a tweed cap?" Argyle bobbed his head harder.

"I think you are trying to tell me something. What is it, Argyle?"

Argyle snorted and dropped the cap in front of Glenn. He flapped his wings and walked around the cap.

"Okay, old friend, I gather you want to me look inside this hat. I see there is a name... the name of the owner. Prádraig Knez of Donegal."

Argyle flapped and growled. He was becoming frantic.

"Stop! Stop! I am listening. Are you telling me that Prádraig Knez is someone I should know?"

Argyle danced. He sang like a muted chainsaw.

Glenn was surprised by his friend's reaction. The bird was obviously excited that Glenn had understood his message. Perhaps, the lady Mysti was answering his prayers.

Glenn settled himself on a rock ledge and thought back to the day of the serpent attack. He remembered that the man who had helped him had a bit of an Irish accent. He also remembered that Argyle was not afraid of him.

Glenn decided that the Lady Mysti was sending a message through Argyle. He had wasted enough time thinking about finding his daughter. Now, it was time to actually get her and bring her home. He would swim to Donegal the next day.

Glenn slept fitfully that night. Questions flooded his mind. Could Argyle be right? Would the cap lead to his finding his beloved Rylee? Would she remember him? Was she being treated well?

Being a considerate son, Glenn thought it best not to tell his and Muriel's parents in advance of his leaving. He did not want to get their hopes up and he knew that Proteus and Irwyn would fight to accompany him. That, he did not want. Finding Rylee was a solo quest. He would travel to Donegal by himself.

He wrote a note telling his parents he needed a change of scenery. He lied and said that he would be gone only a few days. He hated not being truthful with them, but his lies sounded like truths when he thought about the possible outcome of his journey.

COMING SOON!

FOUND KNIGHTS LOST DOWN UNDER

"The undercurrent of my every thought:
To seek you, find you, have you for my own."
~ Edna St. Vincent Millay ~

There was fear in the valley.

Off the Dingle Peninsula in the deepest waters of the Atlantic Ocean lived a tribe of Merfolk. These peaceful water-dwelling souls were known as the tridents of Wading River. While normally a convivial society who valued their elders and cherished their children, they had often dealt with traumas of a kind unknown to humans. These traumas brought great emotional suffering into their lives. They also helped to make them a strong and resilient people.

At the time of this story, a tribe of Merfolk were fearing for the safety of one of their own - an innocent child unable to defend herself against those who might do her harm.

Glenn's parents, Proteus and Salacia, had been roused from sleep by a sense that something was wrong. Their fears had been realized when they found a note from their son stating that he needed a change of scenery and was going away for a few days.

Glenn had only recently recovered from life-threatening injuries suffered during the sea serpent attack that had killed Muriel, his wife, and which had led to the disappearance of his daughter.

Proteus and Salacia knew Glenn was going in search of Rylee. They, too, wanted to search, but they preferred a more thought out plan. As loving parents, they were worried about their son's health. While Glenn felt he was back to his former self, they knew his body was not the only part of him that had been injured. Glenn's heart and soul were shattered by Muriel's passing and the initial empty searches for Rylee. Every night, Proteus and Salacia heard him crying and calling out in his sleep.

During Glenn's recovery period, his parents and Muriel's parents — Irwyn and Mirasol — had kept discreet tabs on his whereabouts. They knew that he visited Muriel's resting place every day. While there, he spent time meditating near the statue of the Lady Mysti... the name engraved in the base upon which the statue stood. Neither set of parents understood the importance of the statue in Glenn's life, but the person she represented seemed to have a calming effect on him.

Much to their concern, Glenn began swimming farther from home and moving with increased speed. His only physical reminder of the serpent attack was a scar on his fin and a slight hitch in his swimming.

The day before his trip, Glenn had gone to the cave that had been a special place for he and Muriel... the one where they had spent their wedding night. That cave was near to where the sea serpent attack had played out. Whenever Glenn visited the care, he became emotional. His suffering was always eased by the arrival of his friend Argyle, a puffin who seemed able to communicate with Glenn on a spiritual level.

While at the cave, Argyle showed Glenn a tweed cap that he had found on the floor. The cap had the name Pradraig Knez embroidered in it. It had been made in Donegal, Ireland. An animated conversation with Argyle convinced Glenn that the key to finding his daughter lay in locating Pradraig Knez.

It was only after a fitful night's sleep that Glenn decided to go to Donegal and find the cap's owner. That was also when he decided to make this trip on his own. Much thought was given to the note he wrote to his parents. Hopefully, his words would ease their concerns about his solo quest.

When Irwyn and Mirasol arrived at Proteus' and Salacia's home for a visit with their son-in-law, they were alarmed to see their friends so distressed. Struggling to keep control of their emotions, Proteus and Salacia explained the reason for their concern. Not knowing Glenn's destination, the four parents agonized over how to proceed. His secrecy was going to make finding him an unfathomable task.

While all involved wanted nothing more than to see father and daughter reunited, they also wanted no more disappearances, injuries or death. Neither set of parents were happy with the choice Glenn had made.

CHAPTER TWO

"Earth and sky, woods and fields, lakes and rivers, the mountain
and the sea, are excellent schoolmasters, and teach of us more than
we can ever learn from books."
~ John Lubbock ~

*A*s Glenn swam north along the coast of Ireland, he
recognized the names of many of the towns he passed
along the way. While he had never visited them, he had heard
about them and read about them as he grew from young boy to
manhood. Never before had he traveled so far from Wading River.
The journey was both exciting and frightening. Glenn did not
know whether to feel elation or sadness. Both seemed appropriate,
and he saw no need to separate one from the other.

Glenn knew when he had crossed into the Blasket Sound by the
chill of the water temperature, the strong tide and the uneven
seabed beneath him. He had taken but a few strokes when he saw
the wreck of the *Santa Maria de la Rosa*. The elders of the community had talked of this vessel, which was a flagship of the Spanish

Armada, many times. The ship had run aground during an attempt to invade England. It went down quickly when it hit the reef. Of the 64 sailors and 233 soldiers aboard, only one person survived; he was lucky enough to be washed ashore.

Glenn knew the ship had been built in 1586. Even though she had sat on the floor of the sea for centuries, the Santa Maria de la Rosa was still glorious. While most of its 26 barnacle covered cannons were still on the gun deck, a few were scattered on the ocean floor. Glenn suspected that not all of the damage to the Santa Maria's hull was caused by hitting the reef. Some was surely the result of doing battle with the British Navy in the English Channel.

Despite its ignominious end, there was no doubt that this barque was once a ruler of the seas. Glenn longed to examine every inch of her, but he was on a mission and must save his explorations for another day.

At Muriel's funeral, he had made a silent promise to his wife, "I will bring our daughter back to Wading River." No one... not Glenn, nor his parents, nor Muriel's parents would be denied the presence of their beautiful little girl. No matter how long or how difficult the task before him, he would bring Rylee home.

ABOUT THE AUTHOR

Rose Tangredi is an emerging author. She grew up in a little seaside hamlet called Wading River in Suffolk County, New York - on the north shore of Long Island. She is the last of 10 children and is proud of her Irish heritage, which plays a big part in *Found Knights... Lost Days*.

Coming from a large family gave her many advantages, not the least of which was learning how to deal with crowd control.

Rose moved to Jupiter, Florida, where she still lives near the sea. She shares her quiet life with two cats, TrelMarie and GeorgeElvis.

Made in the USA
Middletown, DE
22 January 2022